The Baroness and Her Wandering Pearls

Another Mystery Tale of Old Baltimore

By

Virginia Stang

Virginia Stang

ISBN 0-7414-1861-4

Published by:

PUBLISHING.COM

519 West Lancaster Avenue
Haverford, PA 19041-1413
Info@buybooksontheweb.com
www.buybooksontheweb.com
Toll-free (877) BUY BOOK
Local Phone (610) 520-2500
Fax (610) 519-0261

Printed in the United States of America

Printed on Recycled Paper

Published January 2004

DEDICATION

To my very good friends of over forty years, Dr. Barry and Sandee Lever. Sandee's encouragement and support helped buoy my first book, and the Jewish peddler of this tale owes his existence to Barry's imagination.

ACKNOWLEDGMENTS

A special thanks to Jean Walsh, Catonsville historian, for sharing many historical notes of the "Village" with me, and for her interest in my literary efforts.

For the Baltimore rowhouse artwork on the cover, I am very grateful to my sister, Natalie Stang Furth, and Ann Crane Harlan.

AUTHOR'S NOTE

Richard Caton and his wife, Mary Carroll Caton, were "real" people, and the founders of Catonsville, Maryland, thanks to a wedding gift of two thousand acres from her father, Charles Carroll of Carrollton. Carroll was a signer of the Declaration of Independence, and one of the wealthiest men in America. The Catons had five daughters. The oldest, Anne, died in infancy. The youngest, Emily, married the English Consul and lived in Maryland. The other three daughters, Mary Ann, Louisa and Elizabeth, married English nobility and lived out their lives in England and Ireland. Louisa eventually became the Duchess of Leeds. The English were quite taken with their beauty and poise and referred to the three sisters as "The American Graces." Elizabeth and Baron Stafford did marry at this time. None of the three sisters had children.

Baltimore, June 1836

Chapter 1   The Peddler

Young Joshua Asher stood in front of his modest home on Lombard Street encircled by his parents and two sisters. Why had they come outside in front of the neighbors to bring attention to his latest work effort? He frowned and grumbled at his family's efforts to hoist a peddler's pack on his broad shoulders. The twenty-year-old boy was already beginning to sweat under the long jacket full of bulging pockets.

More chattering neighbors were gathering, embarrassing Joshua with their questions and advice.

"I want to go back in the house, Father," Joshua begged, dropping the pack on the ground. They each took an end of the four by four foot burden and hauled it inside, shutting the door firmly behind them.

"Oh, you will never be able to handle it, son," his mother cried. "Why did you ever want to try this?"

Joshua gritted his teeth while his father sat in a chair to catch his breath. The two young girls, Sarah and Esther, urged him to stay at home and find another job in the city.

But Joshua had already tried two jobs, and the one he really wanted was overwhelmed with applicants, and he had not been considered at all. It was an outside job and he could leave the dirty city. The Baltimore and Ohio Railroad was constantly moving westward, gaining more passengers and freight all the time. He wanted to learn to be a driver, or the fireman on the locomotive. Something with action and excitement. Instead he seemed destined to walk alongside the tracks with a pack on his back. At least he would be out in the fresh air.

His mother, while complaining of his heavy load, continued to fill his coat pockets. She tucked some sandwiches and water containers into the few pockets that were not crammed with saleable items. Finally she gave him a packet of very fine lace trim to sell that she had made herself.

"I'm ready to put on the pack again," Joshua said with a smile. "Father, will you please help me with it? The supplier told me it would be easier to manage after the first day."

"And every time you make a sale, the pack lightens," Jacob Asher replied, a broad grin on his round face.

Within ten minutes the pack was firmly in place, and Joshua was ready to leave by the back door. His mother and two sisters shed a few tears and hugged him tightly.

"A week of peddling is enough," Judith insisted. "Be sure to return to shabbes for prayer with the family. And remember each evening to find a dry barn to sleep in, and try to make a good trade with a farmer for some supper," Judith continued, following Joshua out the back where she gave him a hearty kiss.

"I'll walk with you to Pratt Street and the railroad tracks," Jacob Asher said. "Always remember to stay near the railroad tracks and you won't get lost."

As he walked alongside his father, Joshua shifted his gait to accommodate his new burden. It was a nice day and he remembered other walks with his father, especially the ones taking them to see the steam engines at the depot. They came to the tracks and Jacob Asher stopped abruptly.

"I will say my goodbye now. Don't be in too much of a hurry. Stop and rest often." The father put his hand on his son's arm. "Your mother has given you enough advice, but remember to be fair to your customers and polite, and take care of yourself and your pack."

Joshua told his father not to worry, then pulled down the brim of his hat, as he turned westward. With a last embrace, Joshua was ready to begin his new adventure.

Living his whole life in the city, and never having ventured out of it before, Joshua had learned in school what a diverse place Maryland was. If he could get almost to Frederick, he would see the Blue Ridge Mountains in the distance. If he went north or south, there were great cities, but probably just as dirty as Baltimore. To go beyond the

Baltimore Harbor and the Chesapeake Bay, would bring him to a place called the Eastern Shore; good, flat farming land. Then suddenly there was the Atlantic Ocean with its sandy shore, and beyond that, foreign lands. What a lot to see!

Now he must make his father proud of him. The first job after school had been in his uncle's clothing store where Jacob Asher also worked. Two older relatives supervising him, and breathing down his neck, made Joshua uncomfortable. Next, a short stretch as a dishwasher in a hotel was not to his liking. That didn't last long. So here he was, trying a job outside where he could hike through the country in the fresh air and see new territory. If he did well as a peddler, he could buy a horse and cart, then later a small country store of his own in a pleasant town that he might discover along the way.

Joshua heard a whistle, then the sound of the steam engine in the distance. It was coming closer behind him, and he hurriedly stepped wide of the tracks, and stood under a tree waiting for it to pass. It was a small passenger locomotive, with men holding onto their hats, and hanging on the outside of what looked like stagecoaches. Women waved to him from inside. On top of the coaches in the open air were seats filled with passengers protected from the weather by colorful awnings. They all looked so happy. Someday, Joshua promised himself, he would save some of his earnings to ride with them. The locomotive passed quickly and Joshua's load on his back reminded him of his purpose in the country.

There was a great demand for all sorts of goods in the rural areas of Maryland, and the usual route was from Baltimore City going west to Frederick. Passing through Relay, Catonsville, Ellicott's Mills or other towns along the Baltimore and Ohio Railroad or on the Frederick Turnpike, a sixty-two mile long toll road, one was always close to the twisting Patapsco River that emptied into the Chesapeake Bay. This was supposed to be the distance he should cover within the week and be home with an empty pack. He would have to walk a little faster.

Joshua was coming upon a cluster of four houses near the railroad. He knocked at the door of the first house, which was answered by an old man who promptly shut the door in his face. Joshua approached the second house, and after a few moments, the door was opened by an older woman with a plain face who was wiping her hands on her apron.

"So, what do you have in your pack, young man?" she asked wearily.

Joshua quickly went through his inventory list; pins, needles, eyeglasses, buttons, buckles, ribbons, thread, crochet hooks, knitting needles, small pots and pans.

"Yes, I could use a new pair of eyeglasses. Where are they?"

Joshua slipped off his pack and opened his coat, revealing all his treasures. From one pocket he handed the woman six pairs of glasses. After trying them all on and discussing prices, she decided on one pair.

"Stay here on the porch while I fetch my purse," she told him, returning inside the house.

Another woman next door stood on her front step, waving Joshua to come to her. After he had his money for the glasses, he dragged his pack over to the next house.

"I'm very low on buttons," she said.

Joshua pulled a large box from his pack, and sat on her step to rest while she lingered over her selection. When the sale was completed, he worried about getting the pack on his back again.

The woman eyed the peddler closely. He was an attractive boy; dark hair and eyes to match, and a little uncertain of himself.

"You're new at this, aren't you?"

"Yes, ma'am. This is my first day."

"Could you use a drink?" she asked kindly.

"No, thank you. I carry some water in a container in my jacket."

"Sit on the bottom step and put the pack on the top step. Just back into it."

Joshua obeyed and hoped that all his customers had a good set of steps. The woman watched him go to the last house. She hoped the little minx who was a trial to her family wasn't at home. Alas, the girl opened the door when Joshua knocked. Good luck to him!

The young girl with a ribbon in her brown hair looked Joshua over from head to toe as she threw back her shoulders, pushing forward her barely covered breasts. She had Joshua repeat his whole inventory while she devoured him with her eyes. Joshua knew his face was betraying his embarrassment. He waited uncomfortably while she tried to decide what she might want.

"I need some new shoe buckles. May I see what you have? You can come into the house if you like. No one else is home."

"No, thank you, miss," Joshua said quickly as he pulled the packet of buckles from his pack and handed it to her.

"My name is Belinda. What's yours?"

"Joshua Asher."

"Are you Jewish?"

Joshua stood rigidly before the girl, expecting a possible insult when he said "yes."

Belinda laughed, moving closer to him. "Most of the peddlers are, but they are usually older with long beards. You are a real treat!"

"Miss, if you could make your selection, I need to move on. I have to get to Catonsville before dark," he said firmly.

"Where will you stay tonight?"

"I haven't decided yet," he stammered.

She played with the buckles, deciding on a pair from the packet.

"How much?"

"Twenty cents."

"Come in while I get my money." Belinda laid her hand on his arm, and looked deeply into his eyes.

"I'll wait here for you." While she was inside he could struggle with getting the pack on again. He noticed the house had a decent set of steps.

The girl pouted and quickly went inside to fetch the coins. Joshua noticed the woman next door watching them through her window.

Belinda returned and thrust the money at him. "Will you be coming back this way soon, Joshua?"

"Probably so," he lied, immediately deciding he would find a detour. "How far do you think Catonsville is from here?"

"About three miles. You have plenty of time before dark."

"Good. Thank you for the sale." He tipped his hat at her and resumed his journey along the tracks. When he was certain he was out of sight of the houses and Belinda, he decided to sit under a tree and have some water and one of his mother's sandwiches. Well, he thought, he should do better coming into a town; more houses, and he would have to venture onto the turnpike for a long distance although his father was leery of it. Joshua had been told that he would have to pay tolls, that the road was hopelessly inadequate to handle all the travelers, and he would run into more competition, and unsavory people.

He heard the whistle again, and a larger steam engine carrying some sort of freight came from the west and quickly passed him. He wondered what was in the "burden" cars filled with large packs. Ellicott's Mills was now quite industrialized situated on the surging Patapsco River. It was a huge business moving the products of the mills to Baltimore and beyond. He daydreamed of the life of a driver as he finished his meal, then fell asleep in the shade of the tree.

Joshua slowly opened his eyes as he heard the sound of frenzied laughter, shouting, and the yowling of an injured animal. How long had he been asleep? He tried to jump up, but forgot about the pack on his back and rolled over by the tree instead. Running through the meadow were two young

6

boys, each with a handful of small rocks, chasing a small tabby cat while flinging their instruments of torture. The cat ran straight to Joshua who was now standing on his sturdy legs.

Joshua called to the boys to stop the attack. They stopped dead in their tracks, turned and ran into some woods. The panting cat came to the peddler and coiled himself around his feet. Joshua stooped and stroked the animal, looking for any wounds. The cat seemed to be all right except for a few scratches, but perhaps he needed some water and food. Joshua poured some water from his container into a cup from his jacket, and gave the cat some pulled apart pieces of a sandwich. The animal lapped the water quickly, and ate hungrily. Joshua hoped he had a home and would return there unbothered by the cruel boys.

Seeing more houses ahead, Joshua patted the cat on the head, and headed west. He had a lot of time to make up. After several paces, the peddler turned around to find the cat on his heels.

"Go home, kitty. The boys are gone. You can't come with me." But the cat followed him, stopping with Joshua while he made sales at houses. He offered the cat to people along the way, but there were no takers. By the time he approached Catonsville a few hours later, he had bestowed a name on the tabby, Rocky.

Outside of the town, there was one street of houses ending in a heavily wooded area with a dirt road and wagon tracks disappearing into the forest. Joshua made some good sales along the street, enough to catch him up to close the day. He was curious about the dirt road and thought he might wander through the woods a bit to see where it led. As soon as he was away from the street, he felt completely enveloped in the tall trees. He caught glimpses of color that were gaily painted covered wagons drawn around a small campfire in a clearing.

Gypsies! He had heard about them; their thievery, tricks and cruelty. He mustn't linger here. Joshua turned abruptly,

Rocky by his side. But he came face to face with a burly man with a large moustache, and a knife in his hand.

"Drop your pack, peddler," he said in a low voice. "What's in there for us?"

As if on cue, figures came from behind the trees and other men, women, and children encircled Joshua and his cat. The boy stood still, but the animal at his feet began to howl.

Chapter 2   The American Graces

No one in the kitchen of Barnum's Hotel in Baltimore City could be unaware of the terrible crash in the basement. Every hanging pot and pan swung about, and a few dishes laden with food ended up on the floor along with stacks of pure white china.

"The wine cellar!" a waiter shouted as several of them hurried to the basement door. They scrambled down the stairs into the cool stone room with the locked door that was only open when liquor or wine was available in the hotel. A high standing rack of the very best champagne of the house now rested on top of a motionless man, soaked and badly cut from the broken bottles. Slipping and sliding, the waiters moved the rack enough to release the man and check his pulse and breathing.

"He's trying to say something," one of them whispered, leaning closer to the victim who couldn't have been more than thirty. Trying to focus on the waiter above his head, all the broken man could manage to say in a weak voice was, "Tell the Baroness…"

"Tell the Baroness what?" Lt. Mark Bennett from the Western Watch House stood over Dr. Meeks as he had done so many times in the past, watching the police physician complete his examination.

"He's not telling anyone anything ever again," grumbled Dr. Meeks. "No name, address, little money, not even a hat so we could see his hat size." The doctor smiled to himself at his little joke.

"None of the help or the manager could identify him," Bennett continued. "That leaves the Baroness Stafford whom I would rather not disturb tonight, but I suppose I have no choice even if it is past midnight."

One of Bennett's officers was making a sketch of the dead man before he would be removed to the morgue. The lieutenant wondered if this was an accident or a murder. No other person was seen in the wine cellar, but there was a door and steps leading up to the street from the basement that was used for deliveries. The door was found unlocked. How else would the victim have entered? Why was he there? Had another person been with him or followed him inside?

A Gala was now over in the hotel's largest banquet room. The occasion was the American celebration of the English marriage that had taken place last month in London that gave Elizabeth Caton of Catonsville, Maryland the title of Baroness Stafford. The bride had brought her new husband to her country to meet her parents and youngest sister, Emily MacTavish and her husband and children. They were all staying at Barnum's Hotel for the night along with Elizabeth's other two sisters, Mary Ann, Marchioness of Wellesley, and Louisa, Marchioness of Carmarthen, each also endowed by marriage with a noble title. In Europe the three beauties were known as "The American Graces." In Maryland they were simply the Caton girls, granddaughters of the late Charles Carroll of Carrollton, signer of the Declaration of Independence and one of the richest men in America.

Richard Caton, the father of the girls, was a handsome Englishman who had swept Carroll's daughter off her feet. Unfortunately he was penniless, but with a wedding gift from his father-in-law of two thousand acres, he had managed to establish the village of Catonsville. Mr. Carroll had reluctantly consented to the marriage of young Polly to a man he was afraid might end up in debtor's prison.

Lt. Bennett said he would go upstairs to wake the Baroness. The manager of the hotel, Mr. Vernon, protested this idea.

"Can't this wait until morning, Lt. Bennett?" he asked in an agitated voice. "We must keep this as quiet as possible. Will it be in the newspapers? It will be terrible publicity for the hotel."

"I can't help that," the lieutenant argued. "I have to investigate this matter now."

"How often do we have such prestigious guests? You want to take a Baroness and probably the Baron into the basement in the middle of the night to view a dead body covered in glass and champagne? Please wait until morning and take them to the morgue when they are refreshed and the victim is cleaned up."

Bennett sighed. Perhaps the manager was right. "What time will the aristocrats be checking out tomorrow?" The lieutenant had never had to deal with titled people before. His sarcasm was not lost on Mr. Vernon.

"The family will be leaving at noon."

"Very well," Bennett replied. "We will leave them in their beds. I will return about ten and send a note to the Baroness requesting an interview with her. Is that satisfactory?"

The manager breathed a sigh of relief. "Thank you, Lt. Bennett. Everything will be back to normal here sometime tomorrow."

The lieutenant returned to the wine cellar. It was fortunate that the outside entrance was there to remove the body without carrying it through the lobby. The doctor left and Bennett arranged for two officers of the watch to be on guard through the night while some of the waiters were kept late to try to clean up the incredible mess. When the lieutenant was certain there was nothing more he could do until morning, he left the premises.

Outside on the street, Bennett walked to his house, knowing that his wife, Katherine, would be restless until he joined her in bed. Katherine was lovely, even in her eighth month of pregnancy. He glanced upward at the stars, passing a few officers of the watch. He had never known such happiness; owning their own home, having his adopted son, Jeremy, then the new child on the way. He was so content it frightened him sometimes.

Bennett wondered about the dead man in the wine cellar. What connection could he have with a woman like the

Baroness who had lived abroad most of her adult life. She had only been on our shores for a few days and those days surrounded by her new husband, her family and American friends. There had been stories of the Caton girls returning to Baltimore in the newspapers, of the elegant Gala celebrating the new marriage. They were reputed to be such beauties. It would be interesting to meet the Baroness in the morning and perhaps he might also see her sisters. What a good story he would have to tell Katherine who would probably want to know about their clothes, jewelry and hairstyles. He wouldn't be much help there.

Bennett would bypass the Watch House for now. It would be customary for him to return to his office and begin a report of the case for his captain, but instead he would go in early before returning to Barnum's. The report would be on Captain Campbell's desk first thing in the morning. He could envision the man sitting there with an evil cigar in his mouth, his head surrounded by a cloud of smoke. He would read and grunt his way through the report.

Bennett had an immediate reply to his note in the morning as he waited in the lobby. He was invited to the Stafford suite on the second floor. The door was opened by a person presumed to be the Baron's valet. He announced the lieutenant to a couple standing near the fireplace. The newlyweds came forward and inquired as to what they could do for the policeman.

Mark Bennett was at once struck not only by the dark beauty and poise of the Baroness, but her friendliness and interest. Her husband of medium build, with dark blond hair and pale blue eyes, stood beside her, and listened carefully to the lieutenant's story.

"You want to take Lady Stafford to a morgue?" the Baron asked incredulously.

Bennett felt a little foolish telling the Baron that he was also invited.

"I'm afraid your wife is the only lead we have to check his identity. Obviously there is some connection. It seems to me that the victim was trying to warn her of something." The lieutenant glanced at the Baroness who had a merry look in her eye as she replied that she had no objection to the police request.

"I've never been to a morgue before. Would there be other bodies? Perhaps my sisters would like to accompany us."

"Elizabeth!" Her husband was shocked. "This is not a social outing."

Bennett quickly said that their presence would not be a bad idea in case the man had been on the ship from England. Others might have noticed him including her sisters and their servants.

"Do you have a lady's maid, Lady Stafford?" He was glad to know now how to address the bride. As for the Baron, he would rely on "Sir."

"Yes, of course. Her name is Becky Cunningham and has been with me for a year. She is young, only eighteen."

"Other than your husband, I suppose she is closest to you?"

"In other words, this man would know about Becky, and Ridley, the valet, and they might be of some help for identification if he has been hovering around us on the ship or here at the hotel?" the Baroness asked. "Ridley won't be a problem, but I do think Becky might be frightened in the morgue."

"Well, let it be," said Bennett. "Could you come with me now? It is only a short distance. I have a carriage outside. Then I believe you are going on to Catonsville for a visit?"

"Yes, to Castle Thunder to visit with my sister, Emily, then to Brooklandwood in Greenspring Valley to spend some time with my parents."

Bennett was taken aback. He had never heard of a castle in Catonsville.

The Baron broke into the conversation. "Lt. Bennett, do you suspect my wife to be in any danger?"

"I certainly hope not, but why would he want to contact Lady Stafford?"

"I'm sure I don't know," the Baron said as he turned to his wife.

"Must you take Louisa and Mary Ann?" The Baron was irritated.

His Baroness smiled. "Didn't you understand what Lt. Bennett was saying? They might have seen the victim. They wouldn't want to miss it, my dear." She turned to the lieutenant. "May we have half an hour to get ready?"

Bennett nodded, and the Baron slowly shook his head as his wife left the suite to inform the others. "The three sisters are very close. They might as well have been born triplets."

It was another hour before Lt. Bennett could get the group into two carriages for the short trip to the morgue. The husbands of the two Marchionesses had remained in England because of business matters so all three sisters rode in one carriage. The Baron joined the lieutenant along with Becky Cunningham, Lady Stafford's maid, and Ridley, the valet. Becky had agreed to go, wanting to be helpful.

The resemblance between the three sisters was amazing, thought Bennett. All three possessed perfect full bosomed figures with pale alabaster skin. Each had a mass of dark curly hair escaping from their bonnets, and large, expressive brown eyes. They were friendly and full of charm. In contrast, young Becky was blonde, blue-eyed, and apprehensive.

At the morgue, they were met by the attendant who led them down the steps to the cool basement; dimly lit with three tables holding covered forms. The attendant went to one table on the end and uncovered the head of a man with dark hair whom Bennett remembered as the victim. There was a collective intake of breath, and a gasp that undoubtedly came from the throat of Becky.

"Please move closer to get a good look," the attendant said.

Several nasty gashes were on the victim's face with one running into his scalp. The wounds were purple, the eyes closed.

14

The lieutenant looked inquiringly at the group who surrounded the table. All seemed uncomfortable and glanced at one another with distaste. This was clearly not their world.

"Have any of you seen this man before either on the ship or here in Baltimore?"

Five shook their heads in unison while Becky nodded.

"At the hotel," she whispered. "Yesterday afternoon, on the second floor hallway. He passed our suite."

"And what did he appear to be doing?" Bennett asked.

"Looking for a certain suite," Becky said in a stronger voice. "I was coming out into the hallway to fetch my lady some extra pillows from the chambermaid. He glanced at me and went on."

"I won't keep you here any longer," said the lieutenant. "We will return now to the hotel."

Bennett rode with the three sisters in one carriage, sending off the others in the second carriage.

"What comes to my mind is that this may be a possible robbery attempt. You ladies have certainly brought a good deal of jewelry with you from England, have you not?"

"Yes," answered Lady Stafford, "but mostly it is in the manager's safe at the hotel. Except for what we might be wearing, of course."

"How do you intend to safeguard your jewelry when you are visiting relatives in the next few weeks?"

"Both houses we intend to visit have safes," chimed in Louisa.

"Before you leave the hotel today, please go over all your precious items and make sure nothing is missing. I will wait in the lobby until you complete the task. Then you may leave for the country."

While the sisters were in their suites, Bennett took a quick turn about the hotel, checking where the entrances were, the kitchen setup and again the basement area. The wine cellar was restored to its original purpose although only a few bottles of champagne were found in the standing and partially damaged wine rack. The stone floor was stained with the contents from the bottles, and some bloodstains, and the room reeked of alcohol. The two policemen Bennett had left on guard through the night had reported to him earlier in the morning. Nothing had been found that might be considered a clue.

The lieutenant returned to the lobby with a newspaper under his arm and found a comfortable chair. He was ready now to read the latest news, possibly a social item on the Gala last night. The manager approached him anxiously and gave him a message that Lady Stafford wished to see him upstairs. When he went to the suite, all three sisters were there, and also Mr. Ridley and Becky Cunningham. No one looked particularly happy, Bennett noticed.

"While my sisters tell me they have found nothing amiss in regard to their jewelry collections, I have found a leather case with the lock broken and a very valuable black pearl necklace missing," Lady Stafford informed the lieutenant with a frown on her face.

Becky began to sob, and the valet seemed ill at ease.

"And who handles your jewelry besides yourself, Lady Stafford?"

"Becky and whomever might be in charge of the hotel safe, which seems to be the manager. I take cases in and out of the safe, and I have to admit I am occasionally careless, leaving something out on the dressing table, but only for a short time." She glanced with sympathy at Becky. "I am blaming no one but myself."

"I will have Officer Cavanaugh speak with the manager after you sign a complaint that you have lost a piece of jewelry at the hotel. I must have a better description and the value of the lost item."

"Excuse me, Lt. Bennett," said the Baroness. "Becky, do you think it might be possible that one of us forgot to return the pearls to the safe when we retrieved the diamond tiara and necklace?"

"I don't remember returning the pearls," Becky sniffed.

"Nor do I," Lady Stafford admitted. "This is entirely my fault."

"Oh, my lady, you wore them earlier in the day, and we were so involved in taking out the gown and the diamonds for the Gala. And that man who was killed must have been outside the door."

"That must be it, Lieutenant," said the Baron. "When he saw an opportunity, he entered the suite and stole the pearls."

"Then where are they now?" Bennett asked. "Were they stolen from the victim?"

"I don't know, Lt. Bennett," the Baron answered in exasperation. "We need to leave the hotel. This is now police business."

"Quite so, Sir. Have any members of the family left yet?"

"Lady Stafford's parents, Mr. And Mrs. Caton and her sister and brother-in-law, Mr. and Mrs. MacTavish. They wished to return to Castle Thunder early to prepare for our visit."

"Is everyone else still here staying at Castle Thunder?" Bennett asked.

"No," answered the Baroness. "There are not enough accommodations for the servants. They will be staying at the Piedmont Hotel in the village."

"Well, you may all leave after Lady Stafford does what I have asked. We will bring along Miss Cunningham and Mr. Ridley to the Piedmont Hotel this afternoon. Just as a matter of form, we must inspect their baggage before leaving this suite, and take a brief statement from them."

Mr. Ridley stiffened, but said nothing while Becky wiped the tears from her eyes.

"Please don't let this episode spoil your visit. You may be certain I will keep you informed as to our progress in the investigation wherever you are. In turn, if you have any information, please contact me at the Western Watch House. There are many stagecoaches daily on the Frederick Turnpike and a message should reach me the same day." He looked over the travelers, all anxious now to leave the city. "I wish you a safe and pleasant journey." He turned his attention to the two servants without the slightest idea of how he was going to solve this case.

At the Western Watch House, Captain Campbell was waiting for his lieutenant to return from Barnum's and bring his report up to date. The Mayor was certain to be upset at this crime! Officer Blair burst into his office with a message from Lt. Bennett that he was going to Catonsville.

Chapter 3 Catonsville

Joshua picked up Rocky, trying to soothe the cat. The howl turned into a hiss directed at the man with the knife who glared at the intruders. An old woman came from one of the wagons and called out in a strong voice.

"Anton, do not touch the boy or the cat."

The man moved a little closer to his captives, brandishing his weapon while Rocky's green eyes gleamed and the hiss became fiercer.

"I'll skin the cat alive and throw him into the stockpot for supper! Then we will see to the pack."

The woman, barefoot and gaudily dressed, wore gold earrings and many gold chains. She made the sign of the cross as she walked over to Anton and told him to put his knife away.

"Don't you understand," she said in a raspy voice, "the cat is protecting the boy? It will be a curse upon us if you touch either of them."

Anton grumbled and reluctantly replaced his knife in his belt.

"Perhaps the boy would like to pay us a toll for entering the woods and our camping ground."

Joshua remained silent as he stroked the cat who now only issued an occasional hiss. The woman stood between Anton and Joshua, carefully watching the eyes of the cat. She spoke quietly to the peddler.

"Turn in the direction from which you came. Leave the woods and stay inside a building tonight. You are just upon the village. Find shelter soon."

"Thank you," Joshua replied in a low voice to the woman whose eyes had softened. "I will do exactly what you say." With his heart beating like a drum, he turned and retreated down the dirt road, clutching his cat to his chest. He looked back once, but no one was following him. Back on the street where he had made his sales, he finally breathed a sigh of relief and walked to the Frederick Turnpike.

Catonsville sat on high ground surrounded by valleys. It was a way station on the turnpike, known for its cool, fresh air and excellent water supply. Joshua walked past a few stores and businesses and saw ahead of him a two story stone building on a corner with a sign proclaiming it as the Piedmont Hotel. There was a shed and a stable behind the building and maybe he could work something out with the owner for a night's stay inside in return for manual labor or stock. Rocky might have to stay in an outbuilding. Joshua still had some of his mother's sandwiches left for their supper and water to drink.

Several coaches were coming and going and discharging or taking on passengers before the front door. Joshua found the back door, tucked Rocky into his coat, hopefully unseen, and knocked. An elderly man in an apron answered, looked over the boy carefully, and listened to his needs for the night. The man was harried with a more than normal influx of guests for the rest of the week. He could use more help.

"I need a dishwasher in the kitchen tonight. You look sturdy and reliable. There is a cot in a basement room you can have, but that cat you have inside your jacket will have to stay in the stable. Is it a good mouser?"

Joshua smiled. "I only rescued it today. You will have to take a chance on both of us, but I'm willing."

"Good, do you need some supper?"

"I still have some food and water in my pack, but we would be grateful for some breakfast in the morning."

"You will have your breakfast. I'll show you the room, bring you a pail of water to wash up, and take your pack and jacket and lock them in a closet tonight. Agreed?" He held out his hand, and Joshua shook it, then followed the man into the hotel to settle in for the night. After a quick meal with Rocky outside, then putting the cat in the stable, Joshua was ready for an evening of kitchen work.

Lt. Mark Bennett delivered Becky Cunningham and Mr. John Ridley to the Piedmont Hotel late in the afternoon to join the other servants of the Caton sisters. At Barnum's in Baltimore, the Baroness had signed a paper for the hotel manager about her missing piece of jewelry, then given Bennett a written description of the black pearl necklace and set a value in American dollars of $2000.00.

The baggage of the lady's maid and valet had been searched along with the contents of Becky's purse, and Mr. Ridley's coat pockets. The written statements they had made for the police were concerned with their tenure with the Staffords, and any previous employment, and their whereabouts yesterday afternoon. Nothing of any concern to the lieutenant had surfaced.

Bennett wanted to continue up Frederick Turnpike to see Castle Thunder, the nucleus of the village, and perhaps meet Mr. And Mrs. Caton, and Emily and John MacTavish, but he felt that after their journey it would be an imposition. He might make another trip out tomorrow with hopefully some additional information about the missing necklace. If he left the village now he might make it back to Baltimore before dark.

Arriving at the Western Watch House, he wrote a brief report for his captain who had left for home. In the morning he would deliver more details. He was hungry and he wanted to be home with Katherine and Jeremy. Bennett took a hack to Liberty Street. When he entered the house, one light was lit for him in the parlor, and he could hear voices in the basement kitchen. He went down the steps, calling for his wife.

The first person he saw was a small form huddled in a blanket noisily eating some soup at the kitchen table. Jeremy was standing over what appeared to be a very young boy and Katherine was trying to keep from smiling.

"Who is this?" asked her husband, staring at what appeared to be a waif.

"His name is Pat, an Irish lad, and that is all he will tell us," answered Katherine. "Jeremy will tell you the rest."

Mark Bennett asked his wife's ten-year old son for some explanation of the boy's presence.

"I was holding him here for you, Dad," said Jeremy excitedly. "He's a pickpocket, right here on my own street. You need to arrest him!"

Mark Bennett raised his eyebrows, sending a questioning look to Katherine. "Do you know how old he is?"

"I would say six or seven," she answered, "but he will only give us his name."

"What exactly happened, Jeremy?" Mark sat down in a chair close to the boy who ignored him.

"I finished delivering my newspapers, and was standing on the corner waiting for the traffic to slow down so I could cross the street. I felt something wiggle inside my back pocket. I grabbed my pocket and caught a hand with some coins in it when I turned around. It was him, so I held on to his hand, although he struggled with me, pulled him across the street and dragged him into the house."

The boy stopped eating and glanced sideways at the man staring at him. He was blond, blue-eyed and had an angelic face. He was also rather damp.

"Where are his clothes, Katherine?"

"He was rather dirty, so I removed his clothes and washed them. Then I bathed him as best I could," she laughed. "He didn't like the bath at all. Now he is wearing a long shirt of Jeremy's under the blanket." She tilted her head at the boy. "I think tomorrow I will give him a haircut."

"He is staying that long with us? I thought Jeremy wanted him taken to the Watch House tonight. First of all, I want to ask him some questions."

The boy began eating his soup again, oblivious to the others.

"What is your last name, Pat?" No answer.

"Where are your parents and where do you live?" No answer.

"Did you take money from my son?" No answer.

22

"All right. Let's go down to the Watch House for the night. A hard bed in a cell will serve you right." Bennett leaned over the boy in his most policeman-like manner, trying to get some reaction.

Pat dropped the spoon, burst into tears, and ran to Katherine, hiding his head in the folds of her dress. The lieutenant shrugged his shoulders, knowing that the boy understood what was being said to him. Bennett asked his wife what they should do.

"It is dark now and almost bedtime. I will put him to bed with Jeremy and we will deal with it in the morning."

"No," replied an insulted Jeremy. "I will not sleep with a pickpocket, and besides, he might wet my bed."

"One night, son," Bennett said softly. "He will be gone tomorrow. I will start at the Watch House with a missing child report, maybe put his picture in the newspapers. There is always the almshouse. We aren't going to arrest a little child."

To Jeremy's disgust, Pat clung to Katherine all the way upstairs to his bedroom.

The extremely attractive Robert Jamison was the last person to step from the last coach arriving that evening at the Piedmont Hotel. He hoped there was still a room available. He hauled down one piece of baggage and carried a small leather bag that looked like a medical case. He had decided on this particular hotel when he noticed that the Caton servants had tags on their baggage for that destination when they left earlier in the day with an officer of the watch. With his hat worn low over his brow and his coat collar pulled up, he had a few times prowled about Barnum's, usually at busy times when he might lose himself in the crowd, or late at night when the halls were empty. Stepping off the coach, he resumed his normal appearance and was about to pass himself off as an artist, and exert his charm.

There was nothing much he could do about his bandaged left hand. He would still be able to sketch with his right. One broken champagne bottle in the wine cellar of Barnum's had jabbed him deeply as in desperation he had tried to stop his accomplice from confessing their crime to the Baroness Stafford by thrusting the wine rack on his body. So now he had the pearls, but he was after bigger game. The diamond tiara and the matching necklace, a wedding gift from the Baron, could be broken up, unrecognized, sold off in pieces and keep him in funds for life. Where was this jewelry now and also the valuables of the two sisters? In a safe at Castle Thunder in the village. He had overheard this news when the hotel manager conversed with one of the policemen. It was his intent to crack the safe and he had most of the week to get it done. It would take a careful plan. It would help if he could find another accomplice; someone already situated in the house who could be bribed or flattered or made love to like the young blonde lady's maid he had seen in the hotel who served the Baroness. The squeamish John Anders was dead and good riddance. A woman might be the answer.

He took the last room available, but supper was no longer being served. He was directed to a tavern farther up the road that might still be serving light fare. He unpacked and hung up his clothes, then opened the leather bag containing his safecracking tools. In a corner lay the black pearls wrapped in a Barnum's Hotel napkin. He relocked the case and decided to carry it with him to the tavern.

Most of the guests were in their rooms now for the night. He might see the lady's maid at breakfast. He would be in the dining room when it opened. Afterwards, if the weather was good, he would walk up the hill to Castle Thunder with his sketch pad and charcoal, and a small folding stool along with a pair of field glasses. Some plan would present itself, of that he was certain.

Becky Cunningham had a room to herself as did Mr. Ridley, the valet. The other two maids for the two Marchionesses shared a room, were older than Becky and disapproved of her because she was young and pretty. Becky felt very much alone and afraid. What would happen to her when they returned to England if the pearls were not found?

Lady Stafford had said that she blamed no one but her own carelessness, but would she change her mind?

Tomorrow the servants staying in the hotel would leave early after breakfast and walk up the hill a few blocks until they reached Castle Thunder. Tonight they had rested from the excitement of the robbery and the seven mile journey from Baltimore. She supposed the others had rested, but she was in a terrible state, always seeming on the verge of tears. She hadn't tasted any of her food at supper. If only she had someone her own age to talk to. She was desperately in need of a friend.

The window was slightly open in her room; the June air scented and warm. She lay upon the bed in her clothes, imagining all the blame finally descending on her. When back in England, she would be accused, taken to Old Bailey and probably hanged.

The mewing of a cat beneath her window brought her back to reality. She thought she also heard someone whispering. Becky sat up, listened a moment more, then went to the window. A lantern had been lit near the stable door behind the hotel and a young man sat wearily against a tree holding an orange tabby cat. It was as though they were talking to one another. The man was stroking the cat as he spoke to it, and the cat was mewing his satisfaction. Maybe they both might talk to her.

Becky left her room without a second thought, descended some backstairs, went outside and slowly walked toward them. Joshua, exhausted from the long day, stood up, holding the cat to his chest.

"Good evening, ma'am. You ought not to be out here by yourself so late."

As Becky came closer, she realized he was a boy not much older than herself. He must be a worker from the hotel.

"My name is Becky Cunningham and I am a lady's maid, but I have been involved in a robbery in Baltimore with my lady, Baroness Stafford, and I am terribly upset about it," she burst out. "Could I talk with you for a little while?" she whispered.

25

Joshua's half-closed eyes opened wide. "A robbery! Why I was almost robbed myself today by gypsies in the woods. I'm a peddler and this is my first day. I've walked from Baltimore with a pack on my back, made some decent sales, rescued this cat, and helped wash all the supper dishes tonight in this hotel." He slowed the rush of words and sighed. "I'm going to sleep like the dead as soon as I get to my cot in the basement."

Joshua invited Becky to sit with him beneath the tree. Trying to calm down, they talked sympathetically to each other for about half an hour until Joshua had trouble keeping his eyes open, and Becky decided she would be in a lot of trouble if she got caught by one of the other servants out late with this boy.

"Good night, Joshua," Becky sighed and for a moment laid her head on his shoulder. "Thank you for being here. I hope to see you tomorrow."

"Sleep well, Becky. Things will look better in the morning." He kissed her lightly on her cheek. They would go their separate ways now and he didn't expect that their paths would cross again.

Robert Jamison did not sleep well because his cut hand throbbed through the night. Early in the morning, he took off the bandage to wash and shave, and was concerned when he saw a small piece of glass embedded in the wound, which was still partially open. He would have to find a doctor, have the glass removed and the wound sewn. He would ask the manager, Mr. Tyler, when he went to breakfast. Meanwhile he would have to wrap up his hand again with the same linen napkin he had taken from the hotel even if it was somewhat messy. He would keep his hand in his coat pocket while he was in the dining room.

Mr. Tyler directed him to a Dr. Jones up on the hill in a two-story house across the road from the Beaumont property. The next property past that would be Castle Thunder.

Jamison could still carry his art supplies and the case containing the tools and the pearls if he removed his hand

26

from his pocket. He didn't have to go far with the soiled bandage. After his hand was treated, he would continue on to the castle.

The doctor's house displayed his office sign. Fortunately he was starting to see his patients. Jamison only had to wait a few minutes. Dr. Jones unwrapped the hand and asked when and how the injury had occurred.

"I was at a friend's house in Baltimore, and reached for a drinking glass from a high shelf. It dropped to a lower shelf, broke and sent a piece of glass into my hand."

Dr. Jones peered at his patient over his eye-glasses. The young man, who appeared to be about twenty-five, was large, neatly dressed, and rather nice looking with heavy brown hair and deeper brown eyes. His manner was gentlemanly.

"It's nasty. I'll extract the glass, swab it good with alcohol, stitch it up and hope we avoid infection. You will have to come back every day to have it checked and the dressing changed. I will also give you some laudanum to ease the pain."

The doctor noticed the equipment Jamison had brought into the room.

"Are you planning to stay in the village long?"

"Four or five days. I'm an artist and want to sketch some of the impressive homes here."

"Simply walk across the street and there they are; Beaumont and Castle Thunder."

"That is what I have been told. At least it wasn't my right hand that was injured or I couldn't sketch."

The doctor proceeded with the treatment, then wrapped the hand in a clean, white bandage. Dr. Jones studied his patient for a moment as if to make some decision about him. "If you have to leave before the hand has entirely healed, you can have it treated elsewhere. The stitches will have to be removed at some point."

After Jamison left the office, Dr. Jones picked up the soiled linen napkin. In a small corner near the hem, Barnum's Hotel was stitched in pale beige, a shade darker than the linen. The piece of glass from the hand was too thick to be from a drinking glass. It had to come from a heavy jar or bottle. Why was the man lying to him? A cautious man, he decided to save the piece of glass, and wash and keep the napkin.

Chapter 4   Castle Thunder

After Jeremy had left for school, Katherine and Mark Bennett decided to take little Pat to the Western Watch House, have a sketch done to submit to the newspapers, hoping possibly to find his family. Katherine would then take him to the almshouse, where Mark was acquainted with Sister Miriam from a previous case. Hopefully Pat could stay there temporarily. Mark hadn't given Katherine enough time to give the child a haircut. Losing so much of yesterday away from the office, the lieutenant needed to do some catching up.

The Western Watch House on Greene Street was one of three in the city. The Middle Watch House was in the center of town, and the Fells Point one served the eastern end. Pat was hesitant to enter, but Katherine and Mark simply swooped him up, promising him some candy from the market if he sat quietly for the sketch. Mark left them and went in to his office to finish yesterday's report on the robbery at Barnum's Hotel and the death of the man in the wine cellar. The sketch was completed and Katherine left with Pat for the market, and reluctantly the almshouse.

The lieutenant handed his report to his captain who was unusually quiet in his office. Not even his cigar was lit. Bennett returned to his office to see what new cases were there for his attention. Almost immediately Officer Cavanaugh knocked at his door to tell him there was no new information from the hotel manager except that he worried about the bad publicity for Barnum's.

"All the Caton sisters had insurance on their jewelry," Cavanaugh continued, "but the insurance was only in effect in the United Kingdom, not for travel elsewhere."

"That's a low blow for them, but they took the chance."

Bennett told his officer about Pat.

"The captain may not want to bother with the sketch in the paper, sir," Cavanaugh remarked. "Too many street children to make a fuss over, he'll say."

"Will the sketch of the victim make today's copy?"

"Yes, sir. I was wondering how the little lady's maid is doing. She is too young to have the jewelry as a responsibility."

"I intend to check on her later. I don't believe she's involved, although I can't eliminate the valet. This robbery was clever and it took two men. A woman would be unlikely to push a standing wine rack on another person. Where do you suppose the accomplice has gone with the pearls?"

"Bennett!" called the captain, throwing open his office door and startling Officer Cavanaugh. "I have some questions here about this report." He waved the papers in front of his lieutenant. "Come with me." The captain left the room, then stopped a moment to light his cigar. Mark Bennett sighed and knew he was in for a long session. Fortunately there was nothing really demanding on his desk today. Maybe he could go out to Castle Thunder this afternoon. It would be a good idea to check on Becky Cunningham, and try to gather some more information from the sisters and family and whoever else might be there. If his wife was sad about leaving Pat in the almshouse, he could tell her all about the castle. If she wasn't so pregnant, she could have gone too.

Joshua was enjoying a well-earned breakfast in the kitchen of the Piedmont Hotel. He was still tired from yesterday, but was reviving with the bacon and eggs, and brown bread and tea. He would save a small plateful and some milk for Rocky in the stable, then they would be off in the direction of Ellicott's Mills after peddling at some Catonsville houses.

Mr. Tyler, the manager who had hired Joshua yesterday, came to his table with a proposition. "I would like you to stay another night, Joshua, and help like you did last night. You are a good worker."

"But I have to get back to my peddling. I must get as far as I can. I know I can't make it to Frederick this trip, but I have to allow time to return to Baltimore by the end of the week."

"The name of this hotel is the Piedmont Hotel. Do you know what that means?"

"Yes, sir," said Joshua curiously. "Foot of the mountain."

"From now on, you are headed for hilly country. It is going to be up and down all the way. Why don't you stay here one more day, sell your wares here in town and lighten your load?" coaxed Mr. Tyler. "Besides your cot in the basement, I'll give you all three meals today and put up a table on the porch out front so you can lay out your pack."

Joshua liked the sound of that. "I could still do the town and a bit beyond during the day," and to himself he thought he might have a chance to see Becky again. He could even knock on the castle door.

"Good, Joshua. What difference does it make how far you go as long as the pack and jacket are empty when you return home? You go feed your cat and let him out on the porch in the sun. I'll put the table out and get your gear out of the closet."

"Will there be good traffic in town today?"

"Son, this town sits on the Baltimore and Fredericktown Turnpike. You are going to see some real sights today. Better to be on the porch than tramping the road."

"Mr. Tyler, have the Caton servants gone up to the castle yet?"

"They were the first down to breakfast. They've been gone about an hour. Do you know them?"

"No, not really," said Joshua, his face reddening. "I briefly met Miss Cunningham last night."

So, that's how it is, smiled Mr. Tyler. A good-looking young man, and a pretty blonde girl, both about the same age. How quickly they had connected.

Katherine arrived at the almshouse, holding tightly on to Pat's little hand. She knocked at the door and was admitted by a young woman when she asked for Sister Miriam. They were told to wait in a small parlor where Pat started to become anxious.

"Is my mother here?" he asked, tugging at Katherine. "Find her for me."

Sister Miriam entered, dressed in the voluminous black habit and veil, with a large white apron around her waist.

"How nice to meet you, Mrs. Bennett, and isn't this little Pat Tracy with you?"

Surprised, Katherine looked down at Pat who now hid his face in her skirt and started to cry.

"He's been here before, Sister?"

"Yes, indeed, with his mother. There was no father around as far as we know," whispered Sister Miriam. "Mother and son were here with us for several months, oh, perhaps we saw them last about three months ago. Mary Tracy, his mother who is consumptive, decided to leave and move in with a female friend."

"My son, Jeremy, found him on the street, quite disheveled. We took him in last night, fed him, cleaned him up, but he wouldn't tell us anymore than his first name. Of course, he wants his mother."

"Mrs. Bennett, I'm sure Mary Tracy would not unwillingly leave her son alone." The nun lowered her voice. "I'm afraid Pat's mother has probably died from the consumption. Of course, you or your husband, Lt. Bennett, can search the death records now that you know her name."

Stunned, Katherine stared at Pat who was sobbing as he clutched her skirts.

"What am I to do with him, Sister?"

"We can take him for you unless you want to try an orphanage where he would be with other children and not mixed in with adults as we have here."

"But he wants his mother," Katherine said unreasonably.

"You weren't thinking of caring for him by yourself, even for a short time, were you? You have your own baby to think of and care for. When is your baby due?"

"In a month. I do have a son who is ten. He could help."

"I wouldn't count on that, Mrs. Bennett. Have you some woman who can attend you after the birth?"

"We're looking earnestly for someone. My husband is putting a sketch of Pat in the newspaper to see if any family comes forward." Katherine began to shed a few tears, uncertain what to do.

Sister Miriam bent over Pat and tried to release him from Katherine's skirts.

"Do you remember me, Pat? Would you like to come back with us for a while like before?"

"Is my mother here?" he asked the nun as he choked on the sobs.

"Your mother is not here, but I am here and others who will look after you."

Then Pat turned back to Katherine, and clutching her even harder, wanted to know if she would be his mother. Katherine was undone.

"Sister Miriam, thank you for your time. I believe I will take him home with me for a little bit longer until my husband can check the death records and do more detecting about Pat's family that he thinks is possible."

The nun watched Katherine leave with Pat, hand in hand, and walk slowly away. Mrs. Bennett needed rest, not added aggravation during the last month, the nun determined.

Mrs. Jones greeted her husband, the doctor, with a light summer luncheon at noon. News was already buzzing through the village about the arrival of the Caton family the day before. All knew about the lavish Gala and many were hearing about the robbery and murder at the hotel in town. Dr. Jones listened patiently while he consumed his food. He didn't like village gossip, but the incident in the wine cellar made him think about his patient. There was the broken glass, and the napkin put away in his examining room. It made him pay more attention to what his wife was saying.

Jamison, with all his gear, walked across the road. He paused at the first house, Beaumont, and marveled at its size, wondering how many rooms it contained. The house was white and sprawling with a three-sided wraparound porch. Looking ahead to the neighboring house, there were so many leafy, shady trees, he could only catch glimpses of its golden hue through the greenery.

Chapter 5   The Artist

Expecting to find himself in a more pastoral setting, Robert Jamison was taken aback by the commotion on the turnpike. The congestion came from both the east and the west. Mixed in with the Conestoga wagons, stagecoaches, and carriages were horses, pedestrians and livestock. Peddlers, farmers and travelers vied for space along with sheep, cows and pigs. Many traveled as families, loaded down with their possessions. Those who dared to walk on the road sometimes risked their lives.

He came as close as he could get to Castle Thunder which was the edge of the Beaumont Avenue separating the two houses. The Caton house wasn't a castle at all. A long, deep two-storied house of yellow brick appeared as a farmhouse with a wide front porch and a mansard roof. Peach and pear trees were abundant in the rear.

Any entry to the house would have to be tried at night, Jamison knew. There was simply too much activity in the daytime. He didn't need much space for the sketching. First he scanned the area with his field glasses, looking for entrances, and then set up his stool in the shade, and pulled out his sketchpad and charcoal. He could have been a talented artist, but never really took it seriously as he wasn't the starving type.

About twenty minutes later, a man came out of the house and walked toward him. Jamison remembered him from Barnum's all too well. It was the Baron.

"Good morning, young man. So you find the house interesting enough to sketch?"

Jamison stood up, holding his sketch. "Yes, sir. You are the owner? Should I have gotten permission?" He would play this to the hilt.

"No, I am only a guest. Stafford is the name. I don't think you need anyone's permission. You are not actually on the property. May I see your work?"

Jamison showed him the picture, and introduced himself. "I am traveling about this part of Maryland sketching some of the more important houses for an art book," he lied. "After Castle Thunder I am heading for Ellicott's Mills to do the George Ellicott house."

"Quite good, so far." The Baron returned the sketch after a close look.

"Could you tell me, sir, why the house is named Castle Thunder?"

"The whim of a young girl in love with her new husband and new home. That was Mrs. Caton, only sixteen when she married. She was a reader of romantic novels. Probably still is."

"How many rooms are there?"

"Twenty-eight. All the women have gone to morning Mass, and Mr. Caton is still sleeping. Would you care to come in for a moment and see the downstairs? The house has been recently redecorated. Would that be of interest to you?" The Baron was bored in the house alone with the MacTavish children and the servants.

Jamison couldn't believe his ears. "How very kind of you, sir. Thank you." He gathered up his gear, including the leather case, and walked with the Baron to the front porch.

"Leave your things here on the porch. We won't be very long." The Baron noticed Jamison's bandage, but was too polite to mention it.

In the next hour, the artist was shown the public rooms including the kitchen. Jamison's eyes darted about each room, trying to store in his memory entrances and the general layout. Inside the library, he noticed an interesting alcove with a sturdy Gothic door with heavy brass trim. Jamison suspected that this might be the way to the safe. He tried to show an interest in the artwork in the various rooms, and ended up promising to send the Staffords at Costessy Hall in England a copy of his forthcoming book that would never be published.

In the dining room was a flurry of excitement. The grand dining table was being set with fine china, crystal and silver.

"The family is entertaining tonight," the Baron informed him. "I suppose we ought to go outside."

As they went through the hall to the foyer, Jamison caught a glimpse of the blonde lady's maid ascending the staircase. She was carrying an armful of laundry. She looked back and the artist gave her a dazzling smile and a slight bow.

On the porch they found two of the MacTavish children fiddling with Jamison's leather case, and making a mess with some spilled charcoal. He glared at them while the Baron spoke sharply, and the children jumped to their feet and took off for the orchard.

As Jamison thanked the Baron for the tour, and in turn was told to continue with his sketching, two carriages containing the Caton women returned from the church and proceeded up the drive. Jamison hastily gathered up his possessions and returned to his work at the edge of the property, but instead of sketching the outside of the house, he began to reproduce on paper a floor plan of windows, doors, stairs, and the alcove.

Lt. Mark Bennett and Officer Cavanaugh arrived at Castle Thunder just past two in the afternoon. They missed Jamison who had returned to the hotel. His hand was throbbing again, and he took some of the laudanum and decided on a nap. Since the house would be full tonight, he would have to wait until tomorrow night.

The lieutenant was disappointed that there was no castle, only an extremely large yellow brick farmhouse. He was very pleased to meet Mr. And Mrs. Caton, and the MacTavishes who were the present owners. Emily MacTavish, the youngest daughter of the Caton's had inherited the house from her grandfather, Charles Carroll of Carrollton.

When Bennett again met the Baroness, the two Marchionesses, and Emily, it was quite evident that their beauty and charm was a gift from their mother.

"I really have no news to report," Bennett told the assembled group. "The hotel manager believes the murdered man and his accomplice were complete outsiders. All the help that evening throughout the hotel has been cleared and there are no suspicious guest registrations. We are awaiting some response from the victim's sketch that appears in today's paper." Bennett wished he could tell them more. He was afraid that the investigation was going to come to a dead end in Baltimore.

"I was hopeful that one of you could remember something from your short stay at Barnum's. The hotel has a very good reputation," the lieutenant continued. "I would like to clear them entirely. They are extremely upset at the occurrence."

"Well, so are we," sighed Mary Ann, Marchioness of Wellesley.

No one else made a comment. Bennett came back to his original idea.

"You ladies," and he glanced at all the Caton women in turn, "are traveling with a fortune in jewelry. I'm wondering if the thief may not be far behind."

"You believe he would make another attempt to rob us?" asked the Baroness innocently.

"But Lt. Bennett," interrupted Louisa, Marchioness of Carmarthen. "I told you before that this house and my parents' home, Brooklandwood, each have a safe."

"May I please see the safe?" asked Bennett with a frown.

Mr. Caton stepped forward and pulled out a ring with several keys attached. "I and my son-in-law, John MacTavish, have access to the safe here at Castle Thunder. Everything placed in the safe or taken out goes through us."

Bennett thought that while necessary, it sounded like a damn nuisance whenever the women wanted to dress up.

"Come with me to the library," said Mr. Caton.

The ladies waited in the parlor while Lt. Bennett and Officer Cavanaugh followed Mr. Caton to the alcove with the Gothic door. He unlocked the brass-trimmed door and there was an iron waist-high safe standing on the floor. After a moment more, the safe was opened and revealed multiple shelves filled with velvet bags or cases clearly marked with the owner's initials, and a code as to the contents. With so many women in the house, and also some of the men's jewelry, the safe was full to the brim.

The safe was relocked and the men returned to the parlor. Lt. Bennett asked if the family wanted a round the clock guard on duty. It should be worth it to them to hire one. Bennett could recommend someone, but the Catons should speak to their local authorities about it. Declining his suggestion, Mr. Caton said, "It would be a bother to have one more person in the house."

Next, Bennett wanted to know if any loiterers had been seen about the grounds, or any strangers knocking at the doors.

"Only an artist sketching the house by the side of the road," the Baron replied. "I chatted him up. Quite a good artist really. Poor fellow had damaged his hand and it was bandaged, but luckily he sketched with his good hand. I invited him in for a few moments while the women were at Mass. He seemed every inch a gentleman."

"Why would you ask a perfect stranger into my house?" asked an annoyed Emily MacTavish.

"Thought the fellow might like to see the inside of what he was sketching. He's compiling a book of his house sketches and will send us one at home." He glanced at his wife for approval.

His new bride rolled her eyes at him and turned away.

"Did he tell you his name?" Bennett asked.

"Yes, Robert Jamison."

"Did you ask where he was staying?"

"No."

"Did you ask how he injured his hand?"

"No."

"Is he still outside sketching?"

"I believe he left about one." The Baron was becoming bored with the questions.

The lieutenant gave up on the Baron. He was ready to see the lady's maid.

"If anyone unusual comes around or the artist returns, please let me know. Remember you can send me a message by stagecoach to my Watch House. There are eight daily coaches on the turnpike. If you need someone in a hurry, get the local police. May I see Miss Cunningham, please?"

Lady Stafford looked surprised, but went to fetch her. Bennett asked to speak with her in a room apart so he was taken into the library. Becky was standing in the center of the room, looking uncomfortable while fidgeting with her apron. Her cap was askew on her blonde curls. Her pretty blue eyes were lowered.

"Please sit and feel at ease, Miss Cunningham. I know how upset you were yesterday and wanted to make sure that you were feeling better today." He thought her color much improved. Becky sat primly in a straight-backed chair.

The burly Officer Cavanaugh stood in a corner taking notes, and observing her fine figure.

"Lady Stafford has been very kind to me," Becky replied, a smile on her face. "Today, she really doesn't seem too upset about her loss."

"Even if it was a very expensive piece of jewelry? Wasn't there an emotional attachment to the pearls if it was a gift from the Baron?"

"Oh, but it wasn't a gift from him. They were given to her by a former, well, an admirer," Becky blushed.

"I see. So you are settling in well at Castle Thunder?" The girl nodded. "Have you noticed anything here that you might be concerned about?"

"Only the artist who the Baron let into the house. He should be more careful with strangers."

"You saw the artist?"

"Yes, and also at our hotel where he is staying."

"Oh, have you spoken with him?" Bennett exchanged a glance with Cavanaugh.

"No, only saw him getting off the stagecoach with his baggage last night."

"I suppose that's all I have to ask you. I won't keep you from your work any longer." The lieutenant was eager to be off on this meager lead. "Please remember to contact me if anything unusual occurs."

Bennett and Cavanaugh took leave of the Caton family and returned to the Piedmont Hotel. The manager gave them the room number of Mr. Jamison, but didn't know if he was in or out.

Upstairs, Bennett knocked repeatedly on the door, but did not get a response. He didn't think it wise to leave a message. He would have to think of something else. After all, this might be a wild goose chase.

In his hotel room, Jamison had taken a large dose of laudanum and fallen into a deep sleep. He never heard the knocking on the door.

Joshua couldn't believe the sales he was making from the porch of the Piedmont Hotel. All sorts of people came to look and buy while Rocky lay sprawled in a pool of sunlight near his master. The cat watched the peddler intently when someone came too close. It was hard though for him to stay awake in the warmth of the sun.

About two in the afternoon, Joshua decided he needed a break and some lunch. He closed up his pack, wanting to try the road. The peddler went into the kitchen for a meal, then took some food and milk to the stable where the cat had been put. Joshua wondered whether he should take Rocky on the road or let him stay in the stable. He decided with so much congestion on the turnpike, the cat might get lost or hurt, so he left him to take a nap, certain that Rocky would be content after a good lunch.

Joshua picked up his pack and headed west up the hill toward the castle. Even though he was busy, he had thought a good deal about Becky all morning, and wanted to make sure she was calmed down after last night. He liked what he saw of Catonsville despite the busyness of the turnpike. Most of the buildings were along the turnpike surrounded by masses of woodland. Modest log houses, stone houses, and brick houses abounded, mixed in with stores, taverns, hotels and businesses. He heard that on the outskirts of the village, mansions and estates were being built. Soon he would see the castle that must be the finest of them all.

Along the way he went up one side of the road and planned to return on the other to do some peddling. He had good luck along the way while dodging the traffic, and on the top of the hill he was shown by one of the neighbors the yellow building surrounded by trees.

He was disappointed that Castle Thunder was not really a castle. It was a very beautiful house, but there was no resemblance to his idea of a castle. He would go around back to the orchard and knock on a rear door, trying to sell his stock and see if Becky was nearby. Some children were playing in the garden, and workers were tilling a field. He knocked gently at a door. A large woman, looking very flushed, came out, saw his pack and told him to move on. He could smell the aroma of tonight's supper.

Then he asked for Becky. "She is a friend of mine from the Piedmont Hotel. May I please see her?"

The woman looked Joshua up and down, liked what she saw and his manner on second sight, then told him to wait under a tree. He didn't have to wait long. The lady's maid came quickly out the door.

"Joshua, I thought you were leaving Catonsville today," Becky said, surprised and very pleased that he had stopped to visit.

"Good afternoon, Becky," he replied, noticing that there was quite an improvement emotionally since last night. "Mr. Tyler, the manager, asked me to stay over one night more to help again in the kitchen. Three meals today and he let me sell my supplies on the porch of the hotel. Did as well as if I had been tramping along the road."

"Then maybe I could see you again after supper?" she asked, a bit breathlessly.

"Like last night?" he asked in a low voice.

"The servants will be back for supper at the hotel tonight. After I prepare my lady's bath, lay out her clothing, and dress her hair for this evening, we are being sent down the hill because it will be a late night with the guests, and the kitchen will be crowded with the MacTavish help."

"I might not be able to get away until ten o'clock."

"Be where you were last night, and I'll look out my window. How is Rocky?"

"Waiting for me in the stable." He gave her a parting smile. "Do you also turn down the covers?"

"Yes, and I also plump the pillows," Becky laughed.

They looked at each other intently until the spell was broken by the large woman coming out the back door.

"Lady Stafford needs you, Becky."

Joshua quickly hitched up his pack, although he was reluctant to leave. Becky turned and hurried into the house. She could hardly wait to leave Castle Thunder and be with the peddler and his cat at the stable.

Chapter 6 Dilemmas

The sun was dipping below the trees, and people still traveling the turnpike were giving serious thought to where they could find a decent meal and shelter for the night. Inns and hotels were available along the length of the road, and accommodations were needed for horses and farm animals. Some travelers made camp by the roadside at night while decent hotels like the Piedmont offered stagecoach passengers and others clean rooms and meals. The poorer class could find an establishment that did not offer food or a bed, but simply a space on the floor of the main room close to the fire.

Castle Thunder was aglow among the shade trees. The Caton family was ready to welcome a small gathering of their village friends and neighbors for the evening meal. All the elaborate jewelry rested in the safe tonight. The women wore light summer gowns adorned with simple gold or silver pieces; some set with semi-precious stones. This was an informal evening even though the set table in the dining room belied that fact. The main course after the soup and fish was roast beef and gravy with seasonal vegetables, and a variety of hot breads. The cook had outdone herself with a frothy Lady Baltimore cake for dessert. An abundance of wine and whiskey was served before and during dinner, with brandies, sherry and coffee afterwards.

Farther down the hill at the Piedmont Hotel, Becky joined the three other personal servants for a rather dull dinner. Chicken and ham were being featured tonight. It was tasty along with the vegetables, bread and pound cake for dessert. The company was what needed spicing up. The valet and the other lady's maids were usually talking between themselves, excluding Becky as much as possible. She must have been young enough to be daughter to any one of them. She toyed with her food, thinking of Joshua, until she looked up and saw the artist enter the dining room. He saw her at the same moment, inclined his head to her and smiled broadly. Becky gave him an uncertain nod.

Robert Jamison found an empty table next to them, and sat there wondering how he might engage Becky Cunningham in conversation after dinner. The only public place they could be together was on the porch or the small lobby. Either place was unsuitable for his purpose; too many people coming and going. It would be unseemly to try to converse between the two tables in the dining room.

The servants, having been served first, were ready to leave before Jamison had begun his meal. In a rare instance of friendliness, the valet, Mr. Ridley, suggested that the four of them should enjoy the evening air in the rocking chairs on the porch. Becky, for once glad to be in their presence because of the stares of the handsome artist, quickly agreed.

Jamison watched them leave the room, ordered a glass of wine, then concentrated on his food. Perhaps he might ask her to take a short walk. The others could act like chaperones, observing them from the porch, then he and Becky might simply turn a corner and disappear in the dark. He smiled to himself. What a sight he could conjure up! Very early this morning he had circled the hotel buildings and property looking for a quick exit, if needed. He particularly liked the stable. In his arrogance, he was certain he could lure her into the quiet stable, flatter her with some words and kisses, then quickly pull up her skirts, strip off her underclothes, and make love to her in the hay before she could make much protest. Possibly she might enjoy herself. Then he would have her falling in love with him and she could become his accomplice. But time was of the essence. He didn't want to follow the Catons around Maryland.

Jamison paid his bill, swallowed the rest of his wine and left for the porch. He walked across the lobby and stood outside the door, looking for Becky. The four servants, with Becky on one end, their backs to Jamison, were rocking. All four chairs were moving at a reasonable pace, but not synchronized. Jamison stared for a moment, then became dizzy. He experienced a sharp cramp in his stomach.

45

Suddenly his hand was at his mouth and he turned frantically toward the stairs. He made it to his room in time to vomit into the bedclothes. Too late he remembered he was not to drink alcohol while taking laudanum.

Becky and the others were unaware of what was happening behind them. After about half an hour, Becky retired to her room to rest, and wait for ten o'clock for Joshua to appear beneath her window. She picked up one of the cast-off novels of Lady Stafford and read and dozed the time away. Like her mother, the Baroness also liked romantic novels, and even had a few in French that Becky didn't understand, nor the sketches of unusual couplings that appeared on some of the pages. One day, her lady had found her looking at one of the French books in a puzzled way.

"My dear Becky, if your mother could see you, she might think I was trying to corrupt you, but you are eighteen now and moving in a sophisticated world. You are a very pretty girl and you have to be aware of how different men can treat you. Some may be very sincere, others simply out to seduce you and sometimes it is quite hard to tell the difference until it might be too late."

"I've heard of that problem, my lady, but I don't understand some of these sketches." She handed the open pages to Lady Stafford.

"Sometimes, women love women, and men love men, and little children can also be involved and terribly abused. Tell me, have you any interest in anyone, male of course?"

"No, my lady. There hasn't been much opportunity so far."

Lady Stafford laughed. "I can guarantee it will happen soon. Please always feel free to come to me like a mother if you have any concerns."

"Thank you, my lady."

Becky continued to read the romantic novels, but put aside the ones in French.

Now she heard a pebble against her window. She looked out to see Joshua holding Rocky under the stable lantern.

"I'll be right down," she whispered.

They sat together under the tree with the cat draped across their legs. This is what Rocky liked and it forced the couple to move closer together. Becky told Joshua about her interview with Lt. Bennett, and the artist sketching at Castle Thunder. She also mentioned how uncomfortable the artist made her feel while they were all in the dining room at supper.

"He stared at me in the most brazen manner. Have you seen him about? He has a bandaged hand."

"Yes, while I was selling on the porch," Joshua replied. "He came out with a leather case, and I suppose his artist supplies. Later on he came back to the hotel before I left to go up the hill."

Becky's thoughts were turning to a more serious matter. "Are you leaving tomorrow?" she asked wistfully.

"I have to get to Ellicott's Mills or possibly beyond by tomorrow night. That will be halfway through the week. The following day, I will have to begin the journey home. My family expects me home for Friday night services. I'm Jewish, you know."

"Yes, I thought so, Joshua. My lady has some Jewish friends in England. One has written a book. She says he is quite intellectual. Lady Stafford has a great interest in literary circles."

"Well, I'm simply a peddler, striving like so many others to make a living. I really would like to drive a locomotive, but too many want jobs on the railroad." He reached behind Becky and hugged her to him. She laid her head on his shoulder. "So will you be at Castle Thunder tomorrow?" he asked.

"We are going to Ellicott's Mills also. We will all leave by stagecoach later in the morning. Maybe we will pass you along the way," she smiled. "The family will be staying at the manor house of my lady's late grandfather five miles west of the town, visiting relatives. We will be staying at the Cliffside Inn a mile or so before. Do you suppose we could be together again tomorrow night?"

Joshua leaned over Rocky and kissed Becky on the mouth. "Are you going to be there one night?"

"I believe my lady said two nights, then we will return to Castle Thunder and prepare for the visit to Mr. And Mrs. Caton's home in Greenspring Valley."

"We don't have much time left, so I will get up very early in the morning, walk and sell as fast as I can manage, and find the Cliffside Inn by suppertime. Wait for me, Becky."

Joshua picked up Rocky and placed him in the stable for the night. He walked Becky to the back door, then took her in his arms and gently kissed her several times before letting her go. He was pleasantly surprised that she seemed to enjoy it as much as he did.

Lt. Bennett and Officer Cavanaugh arrived back at the Western Watch House before Captain Campbell had left for the day.

"I hope you obtained some information to account for the time it took for Catonsville." He was in one of his grouchy moods. He didn't like investigations that took his officers out of the city. "No reports on the victim's sketch in the paper yet, but then most people are only now getting to it. And Bennett, do you really think it was necessary to put that lost child's sketch in the paper for tomorrow? There are hundreds of lost children on the streets. I only permitted it because your wife brought him in."

"Captain Campbell, Jeremy tried to have me arrest the child because he caught him picking his pocket. He can't be more than six or seven. My wife insisted on keeping him all night, bathing him, and giving him a meal. Her plan is to temporarily take him to an almshouse until we get some response, if any, to the sketch."

"All right!" the captain said, running his hand through his sandy-colored hair, and feeling for something in his pockets. "When you are at your desk, after I leave, read today's paper. Front page news about the Barnum Hotel robbery and the victim being one of the Caton girls, now an

48

English Baroness. At the same time there is a murder committed in the wine cellar of the hotel. What is the connection? Any minute I expect a message from the Mayor who will want details of police progress. So what have you learned in Catonsville?"

"First we visited Castle Thunder, the old Caton home, and spoke with all the family who had been at the Gala. I was shown a safe where the family jewelry is kept and I suggested that they still hire a private guard. Mr. Caton didn't think that was necessary. Then it seems an artist had been sketching the house this morning from the road, and the Baron unfortunately let him have a look inside the house. His hand is bandaged, but we don't know why. We know his name and where he is staying, but he was out when we called at the hotel." Bennett ended his verbal report and waited for a comment from his superior.

"And what else?" Campbell asked impatiently.

"That is all we accomplished in a few hours, sir. The artist may be legitimate, but I would like to know about his hand injury. It is possible that the man who pushed the wine rack on the murder victim suffered some injury himself. One of us needs to return tomorrow and find him, and also possibly the doctor there who is treating his hand which has a sizable bandage. We could bring the artist back to the city for questioning if we locate him."

The captain began gnawing on his fingernail, trying hard to make a decision.

"I wanted you to attend to some matters here, but Lt. Michaels can handle them. You and Cavanaugh need to return. If you find this artist and he gives you any trouble it might require both of you to bring him in. Also check with the local authorities and let them know the situation." He reached into his vest pocket and pulled out a cigar. "I'm going home. Write up your report and leave it on my desk. Report in before you leave in the morning for Catonsville to see if we have any overnight developments."

Mark Bennett trudged home some two hours later, anxious to be with Katherine and Jeremy, and hear what had transpired at the almshouse with Pat. He was also famished, not having had a chance to have any supper. One lamp was lit for him in the parlor, which meant both were now asleep. He took a candle into the basement kitchen and lit a larger lamp on the table. Rummaging around in the larder, he found some bread and leftover roast beef to make a sandwich. He washed it down with a pint of beer.

As he was clearing up the table, he heard slippered feet descending the stairs. He glanced up to see Katherine with her robe wrapped tightly around her very heavy body.

Katherine smiled apprehensively at her handsome husband knowing that in a minute he would be frowning at her. Before he could speak, she blurted out, "Pat is here with us for another night."

"Katherine, you promised to take him to the almshouse," he said in a very tired voice.

"And I did, and Sister Miriam told me that several months ago he had been there with his mother who was consumptive. His name is Pat Tracy and his mother was Mary Tracy. They left to go live with a friend, but Sister believes his mother might have died."

"Would Sister have taken him back?"

"Oh yes, Mark, or suggested an orphanage where there were only children, not a mixture like the almshouse."

"Then why did you bring him home? You know this is not possible."

Katherine began to cry. "Why, he wouldn't let go of me; just clung to my skirts and asked me to be his mother. I thought tomorrow we can put a last name to the sketch and see what happens, and when you go to the Watch House in the morning you might send one of the officers to search the death records to see if Mary Tracy has died."

Mark hated to see Katherine cry. She looked pathetic with her intense deep blue eyes shedding tears and her lovely dark hair tumbling around her shoulders. Even in her condition she looked seductive, and he knew relations weren't possible with only a few weeks to go.

"We'll deal with it in the morning." Mark began to tell his wife about his day in Catonsville; about Castle Thunder which wasn't a castle, about the Caton family and the noble marriages, and finally the search for the suspect artist. When they went upstairs to the bedrooms, they looked in on Jeremy and Pat, fast asleep in bed. Each one was at the opposite side of the bed. Katherine thought they looked angelic. Mark was more practical.

"I see you gave Pat a haircut," Mark sighed. "I know, he doesn't have a mother to do it." He pulled Katherine away toward their bedroom.

Later in bed, Katherine asked him more about the celebrated sisters; the clothes, jewelry and hairstyles. Everything he knew she would want to know, but what he didn't pay much attention to. "I can mostly tell you that they are elegant, spirited and can't hold a candle to you." That seemed to make Katherine happy. They lay in bed spoon fashion.

Mark was minus his nightshirt and Katherine's light nightdress was pulled up above her bosom. Mark kissed her neck as he gently caressed her ample breasts. Then he moved his hand back and forth over the swell of their baby. How it thrilled him when the baby moved and he could feel the kicking of his infant daughter's foot. He desperately wanted a girl. Mark liked to think he was going to get another Katherine to love.

Chapter 7   The Doctor

After morning Mass, the Caton family and the Baron were ready to proceed by carriage to the former country home of the late Charles Carroll of Carrollton. The journey was about eleven miles. Relatives would receive them there for a two night visit.

The MacTavish family would remain at Castle Thunder with their servants. The three "American Graces" would trust their jewelry to the house safe until their return on Friday. This would be a time for casual country pursuits.

Becky and the other personal servants had sent their baggage to the lobby, clearly marked for the Cliffside Inn. They were now having their breakfast in the dining room, and Becky had learned from Mr. Tyler, the manager, that Joshua and his cat had departed quite early.

The night before, after Jamison had been so deathly ill, and the fouled bedclothes had been rolled up and thrown in a corner, he had slept fitfully on a bare mattress with only a spare blanket to keep him warm. When he awoke, his mouth was dry and his stomach still slightly churning. He needed to wash, and go downstairs for some hot tea. He must also open the leather case and make sure the children at Castle Thunder hadn't shaken up any of the contents, especially the black pearls wrapped in the napkin. After he was up and moving about, he would visit the doctor again who would treat his hand. Then he would concentrate on his safecracking plan.

Joshua soon realized what Mr. Tyler meant about the terrain after about half a mile. The turnpike suddenly went downhill, then rose again, and continued this pattern until he was in the Patapsco Valley. The granite rocks on either side of the turnpike had grown to great outcroppings of cliffs, vertical slabs and boulders. Between the rock masses, the railroad tracks ran parallel with the surging river and the turnpike. At a curve in the road, the turnpike went over a bridge on the river, past the first railroad terminus in the nation, and continued up a steep hill through the teeming mill town known as Ellicott's Mills.

Joshua was glad to come to a town again. Sales had been sparse since leaving Catonsville. Houses, inns, and farms were more spread out, and the walk, even with a lightened pack, was not easy. Rocky kept pace with him, but Joshua had to carry the cat for a while after the tabby was chased by a dog. Mr. Tyler had very kindly sent Joshua off with a sandwich and water after an early breakfast. The peddler thought a rest beside the river at the bottom of the town would be a good place to stop for lunch, and possibly see a locomotive pass by. Then he could resume his peddling through town and try to unload at least half his stock. That would bring him halfway through his week. Of course on the return, he would be encountering some of the same people he sold to, earlier. He had come six miles. If he could keep up this pace, he would meet Becky on time.

After Mark had left for the Watch House, and Jeremy for school, Katherine fed and dressed Pat, and waited for Mark's sister Edith to come for a sewing lesson. Mark had lived with his sister and her husband Richard before their marriage. The two women had become good friends and Edith had offered to help Katherine after the birth. Katherine would accept the offer, but she felt she must find other household help too.

Edith and Richard, a surveyor, lived close by, but in five years of marriage, Edith had not produced a child. Lying in bed last night, Katherine had a sudden idea that maybe she could interest them in giving Pat a home. If his mother was indeed dead, and no one came forward from the plea in the paper, she would have to do something other than the orphanage or almshouse. She knew Mark was right when he said keeping Pat was impossible. It wasn't fair to Jeremy who still felt uncomfortable about the boy, and harbored some jealousy. It would only tire her more while she was caring for the baby and trying to get her strength back.

Pat sat playing on the floor with some of Jeremy's old toys and picture books. Katherine had told him a very nice lady was coming and he should say hello to her and shake her hand. She coached him as to how to do this. Pat looked very fine; washed, dressed, and smiling. Please, God, Katherine prayed. Let Edith take a liking to him.

There was a knock on the door and Edith was there with a dress in a clothing bag. While she was able to sew, she wanted to learn some fancy stitches for her new dress. Katherine wanted to tell her about Mark and his new case; visiting Castle Thunder and meeting the Caton sisters. Edith would want to hear all the details. Katherine had not mentioned Pat. That was a surprise.

When Edith came in the parlor, Pat stood up, and with a little push from Katherine, said hello and stuck out his hand to Edith.

"Well, where did this little fellow come from?"

Katherine whispered the circumstances to Edith in the doorway, as Pat resumed his play on the floor.

"Do you intend to keep him if he isn't claimed?" Edith whispered back.

"Mark is very much against it, and he's right. We have our hands full now. I shall have to try to place him."

Edith kept watching Pat, not paying much attention to the fancy stitches, or taking much of an interest in Mark's brush with British nobility. Katherine suggested some tea and biscuits. When Pat started to follow Katherine to the basement, Edith called to him to bring her a picture book. Always willing to be read to, Pat brought her his favorite one. He had not been able to sit on Katherine's lap because of her pregnancy, but he climbed right up on Edith's and made himself at home. As Katherine brought the tea tray, she heard Pat ask his new friend if Edith would be his mother.

After having washed and dressed, Robert Jamison decided to have a look inside the leather case. He unlocked the case and found that the heaviness of his safecracking tools had kept them in place, but the black pearls had spilled out of the linen napkin. Taking the necklace to the light, he examined it carefully and could see no damage. He spread out the napkin and noticed for the first time that there was a faint embroidered name stitched in the corner near the hem. Barnum's Hotel. Wasn't it one of the napkins that he had used to wrap up his injured hand? And where was that napkin now? Left in the doctor's office. He tried to remember what he had told Dr. Jones about the way he had injured his hand. He said it had happened at a friend's house. If the doctor had seen the stitching, he would realize that his patient had lied to him. But perhaps he hadn't noticed it and had thrown the bloodstained napkin away. Jamison wondered where the doctor discarded such items.

He left his case with the rewrapped necklace locked under the bed and went downstairs to the dining room. As he passed through the lobby he saw the familiar baggage belonging to the personal servants of the Catons. Surprised, he glanced at the tags; Cliffside Inn. Where were they going? He entered the dining room and passed them on their way out. All gave him a slight nod, which he returned. He noticed that the blonde lady's maid looked very attractive this morning. Jamison sat and had his tea and some toast and wondered where Cliffside Inn could be. Would the jewelry belonging to the sisters stay at Castle Thunder or was it already packed for the next jaunt? The Caton women didn't stay in one place very long. He decided they would take their jewelry with them.

After Jamison's light breakfast, he asked Mr. Tyler if there was room in the stagecoach bound for the inn for himself.

"No, it leaves in about twenty minutes, but I could get you on the next one, early afternoon."

"Good. I'll do that." He would need the time to pack and get to the doctor's office. "Hopefully I can get a room at the Cliffside Inn."

"I will send a message by this early stagecoach. How long do you want the room?"

"I'm not sure. I will decide when I get there."

"How is your hand, Mr. Jamison?"

"The doctor will look at it, this morning. It feels a bit better."

"It's a quick decision you are making to leave us on such short notice," the manager said curiously.

"I want to continue my sketching in Ellicott's Mills."

"You could get a closer hotel in town. Nice one across the road from the terminus."

"No, thank you. I hear the scenery is quite beautiful around the inn," Jamison said, not having the foggiest idea what he was talking about. He thought to himself if he could obtain a horse and mask, he might become a highwayman and simply rob the sisters' carriage. With his injured hand, though, he would need an accomplice and a serious plan. He laughed to himself. He was a good safecracker if the sisters would only stay in one place long enough to pull it off. The Caton women were simply not cooperating.

He walked up the hill to the doctor's office. He had to wait while a small boy was being treated for a nasty cough. Finally it was his turn and the doctor ushered him into the treatment room.

"Have you experienced much pain?" Dr. Jones asked, unwrapping the bandage.

"Yesterday afternoon, I had to take some laudanum, and at supper I forgot and had a glass of wine. I was very sick."

"I'm sure you were. You could kill yourself that way."

When the hand was unwrapped, the doctor sighed and looked seriously at his patient.

"The bleeding has completely stopped and the stitches remain secure, but I'm afraid I detect some small amount of infection."

All Jamison wanted to do was get the damn bandage off his hand. "I was hoping I could get a smaller bandage on, one that I might be able to cover with a large glove."

"Why do you want to put a glove on? The weather is warm today. That won't help it to heal. I will swab it well with alcohol again and try a smaller covering. You will have to return tomorrow."

"I'm leaving for Ellicott's Mills today. Could you refer me to someone there?"

"Yes, in the center of town, there is Dr. Miller. I will give you his address." The doctor treated and recovered the hand, then wrote down Dr. Miller's address. All the while, Jamison studied the treatment room and watched where Dr. Jones threw his discarded bandage; into a wicker basket which appeared near empty.

"Dr. Jones, the linen wrapping I came in with yesterday belonged to my friend. I was wondering if you might still have it or has it been thrown away? I would like to return it to him."

The doctor hesitated. For a moment he felt a wave of malice directed at him. He cleared his throat. "The trash each night is emptied and early this morning, the trashman was here to collect it. I'm sorry, but it is probably soiled beyond repair."

Jamison frowned and asked the doctor his fee, then settled his account. When he returned to the Piedmont Hotel, the stagecoach had left with the Caton servants, but on arrival had deposited a stack of yesterday's Baltimore newspapers on the lobby desk. Jamison picked one up, paid for it, and took it to his room to read while he awaited the next stagecoach heading west on the turnpike.

Lt. Bennett met Officer Cavanaugh at the Western Watch House where they both conferred with Captain Campbell. No one had any information on the murder victim from Barnum's Hotel whose sketch had appeared in yesterday's paper.

"First thing this morning, I sent a copy of your report to the Mayor and also one to the Justices of the Peace. I hope you get something definite in Catonsville today."

"Could Officer Pierce please see that the surname Tracy is placed on the sketch for Pat and run another day in tomorrow's paper?" Bennett asked his captain, waiting for the sky to fall.

"We can do that for one more day," Campbell answered quietly.

"Then could Officer Pierce check the death records to see if his mother, Mary Tracy, has died within the last few months? My wife found out yesterday at the almshouse that mother and child had stayed there for a short time, but the mother was very ill."

In an unusual docile manner, the captain nodded his head and agreed. After a pause, he asked, "How is Mrs. Bennett today? She looked pale when she was here. The baby is due when?"

"A few weeks, sir. She wants to see Pat Tracy settled as soon as possible." His superior's concern for Katherine explained his temporary agreeable nature. Enough of the pleasantries. The captain was ready to return to the business of crime.

"Take a carriage to Catonsville. Don't depend on a scheduled stagecoach. I want you to leave immediately and find that artist!"

Arriving at the Piedmont Hotel, Bennett and Cavanaugh drew up in their carriage as the early afternoon stagecoach with Jamison aboard was leaving. They went upstairs and knocked on Jamison's door as they had done before. Again, there was no answer. Mr. Tyler came into the lobby as the policemen were coming down the stairs. He explained that Mr. Jamison was no longer a guest.

"Left on that afternoon stagecoach, just ahead of you. Made up his mind in a hurry. If you ask me, he seems to be following the Caton servants who departed on the early morning stagecoach."

"What is their destination?" asked Bennett.

"Cliffside Inn, a few miles west of Ellicott's Mills. Must be about eight to nine miles from here."

"Is that where the Baroness and her family have gone?"

"I don't know, sir," replied Mr. Tyler. "You would have to call at Castle Thunder to find out."

"Yes, we will do that, and I also want to know the name of the doctor who treated Mr. Jamison."

"I sent him to Dr. Jones across the road from Castle Thunder. Mr. Jamison went to see him again this morning."

"Do you know anything else about the man?" asked Bennett.

"No, sir. He said he was here to sketch houses. He also seemed interested in the servant, Miss Cunningham. Another thing, he was sick in his room last night. The bedding was soiled. That's all I can tell you."

"We would like to make a quick search of the room."

"Certainly." The manager went upstairs with them and unlocked the door. Jamison had left nothing except a faint odor from the soiled bedclothes that had been removed.

"Thank you, Mr. Tyler," said the lieutenant as they returned to the lobby. "We will call on the doctor."

Bennett and Cavanaugh rode in the carriage to the top of the hill and entered the office of Dr. Jones. In a momentary lull between patients, the doctor was reading yesterday's newspaper that had just arrived in the village by stagecoach. He was thinking that he should consult the local policeman after he had read the article about the robbery and murder at Barnum's Hotel. He was surprised to find two city policemen on his doorstep.

Yes, he had treated Mr. Jamison for a very bad cut on two occasions; one only a few hours ago.

"I was suspicious of the man because he lied to me about where the injury took place and what caused it. He said it had happened at a friend's house while he was reaching for a drinking glass off the shelf."

"Why did you think he was lying to you?" asked Bennett.

Dr. Jones went to a drawer in a medical cabinet and withdrew a cotton bag. From inside he removed the Barnum's linen napkin and, wrapped in gauze, the piece of glass. He handed the items to Bennett who examined them carefully. Officer Cavanaugh let out a low whistle.

"So now we know he was at Barnum's where he cut his hand, and certainly this glass is from a bottle which could be found in the wine cellar," said Bennett with great admiration for the doctor. "This definitely makes him our man. We must take this evidence with us to Baltimore after we apprehend him." The lieutenant returned the items to the bag.

"How did he behave this morning?"

"The wound has some infection. I treated it again and he wanted me to make the bandage smaller so he could wear a glove. I told him that wasn't a good idea, because of the added warmth. He seemed irritated."

"Did he tell you he had been sick?"

"Yes, he mixed the laudanum I gave him with wine at supper. He was lucky he was only sick. He also told me he was going to Ellicott's Mills and wanted the name of a doctor there. I wrote down a name and address for him. Then he asked me if I still had the linen napkin from the day before because he wanted to return it to his friend, but I told him it had gone in the trash. Do you need to speak with one of our policemen?"

"No. No crime has been committed here, and the suspect has moved into another county. If he should commit a crime in Ellicott's Mills, that is a different story. Could you please give me the doctor's name and address there?"

Dr. Jones obliged, then asked if he should keep this confidential.

"That would be helpful to us, Dr. Jones," Bennett replied. "We know what hotel he is going to and we will be right behind him. Hopefully we can take him into custody today and back to Baltimore. For now, perhaps you might simply read the papers to see what progress we are making. He can't be condemned yet."

"I understand, Lieutenant. I'm glad I could be of some help."

Bennett smiled and shook his hand. "The department is very grateful for your help. We can't thank you enough."

Outside, they left the carriage at the doctor's office while they crossed the road to Castle Thunder. Not knowing that another move had been scheduled, Lt. Bennett and Officer Cavanaugh had to find out where the Caton family had gone.

Mrs. MacTavish greeted them at the door and invited them inside.

"My sisters, the Baron and my parents were unsure whether they would be going to the Manor or not. Someone there was ill, but when that relation seemed to recover enough to be sociable, they decided to go. The Manor is one of the former country homes of my late grandfather."

"How much farther from the Cliffside Inn is it?"

"About two miles. It is only to be a two night visit. I apologize that you were not informed," Emily MacTavish said politely.

"Did they take their valuables with them, or leave them here in the safe?" Bennett asked.

"The jewelry is here, and quite safe."

Bennett had his doubts about that. With only the MacTavish family here and their servants, now would have been an ideal time to attempt a go at the safe. Evidently Jamison thought the jewelry had gone to the Manor.

"In two days time they are returning here?"

"Yes, for another short visit, then off to my parents' home."

Bennett thanked her, then he and Cavanaugh returned to the Piedmont Hotel to send messages back to Baltimore by an eastbound stagecoach.

"We have no choice but to continue to the Cliffside Inn and try to apprehend Jamison there. It is eight or nine miles from here. We will have to stay the night and return to Baltimore in the morning." Mark thought of Katherine and Jeremy. He hated to be away from them and they would worry until he returned.

"I have no one to send word to," Cavanaugh said, anxious to get on with the chase and some excitement. "It will be a good story to tell my lady friend when I return."

So the lieutenant sent a message to Captain Campbell informing him of the situation, and another to Katherine that he should return tomorrow. He would be returning hopefully with the suspect in the Barnum case. He was going to be staying in a very nice hotel, the Cliffside Inn, a few miles west of Ellicott's Mills, and Officer Cavanaugh was with him. He felt completely confident about the outcome.

They stopped at a general store to pick up a few needed items for an overnight stay, then went to a livery stable so Cavanaugh could exchange the horses for the longer journey. After a quick meal at a roadhouse, they were finally heading to the Cliffside Inn on a wild goose chase.

Chapter 8   Ellicott's Mills

Joshua thought about Becky as he and Rocky had their lunch on a large rock by the edge of the river. He supposed she had gotten to the Cliffside Inn by now, or possibly was already at the Manor for the rest of the day in the service of the Baroness. The cat took a cautious interest in some fish moving close to them off the bank of the river, but the rapidity of the water over the rocks was too daunting for anything other than to sit and stare. Joshua was mesmerized by the small whitecaps breaking over the rocks, and the constant hiss of the moving water. It amazed him to see so many houses built on the edge of the Patapsco, certainly a hazard when the river rose.

After they had rested, he knew he must get back to his peddling, but the terminus was so close and so new that he wanted to see it and any new arrivals or departures of the locomotives. No reason why he could not sell out front for a short while before moving up the hill. Joshua spread out his pack on the ground, and found that business was good, and railroad traffic brisk. He hated to leave, but put on the pack once more and proceeded west up the turnpike through town going back and forth across the congested road, trying as many houses and places of business as he could. When he left the valley and reached the top and the terrain leveled out somewhat, he found that sales would again be sparse. He concentrated on getting to the inn, having asked one of his customers the directions.

After two miles, Joshua came to a sprawling sheep farm with a large stone house, barns, and outbuildings. The flock of sheep was large and the new lambs did not venture far from their mothers. The next property was the Cliffside Inn, which was another stone building similar in size to the Piedmont Hotel. Joshua didn't understand why it had that name as he only saw a few small hills surrounding both properties. He would try the inn first, then the sheep farm, for arrangements for the night. Today he had definitely halved his stock, so he was in good shape for the return trip to Catonsville in the morning.

Leaving Rocky on the porch of the hotel with his pack, Joshua entered the lobby and asked if Miss Cunningham had arrived. The manager, Mr. Adams, told him her party had registered and were at the Manor two miles away, but would be returning soon for supper. That was good news. Joshua then asked for a meal and a night's lodging in return for some peddler stock or night work in the kitchen or outbuildings. The manager might have refused, but since the peddler knew a member of the prestigious Caton party, he would give the young man, who seemed quite well-spoken, a job in helping to feed the animals in the stable. Joshua could stay in a small room in the attic for the night, and the cat with the animals.

The arrangement pleased Joshua and he offered Mr. Adams some of his peddling stock and the man took a pair of eyeglasses and a belt buckle. Mr. Adams said he would give the peddler breakfast in the morning. So Joshua settled in, washed, had a good dinner and some food for Rocky. He did what he had to do; feeding the animals and helping with the horses. When he had finished his chores, Joshua waited for Becky to come to him as he sat on a bench with his cat on his lap beneath the stable lantern.

Edith stayed through tea and biscuits, and then for lunch. She attempted to do some sewing, but mostly she enjoyed Pat's company. In the early afternoon as Edith thought about her plans for Richard's supper, a knock came at the door.

Katherine was surprised to see Officer Pierce.

"Is anything wrong with my husband?" she asked anxiously.

"Oh no, ma'am. Lt. Bennett sent me to find a possible death record for a Mary Tracy and report back to you. I regret to say that I did find it. Mary Tracy died exactly a month ago. I also have additional information."

"Oh, please come in, Officer Pierce." Katherine tried to shield Edith and Pat from the conversation. She started to whisper, but Katherine couldn't control her trembling.

"Who supplied the information and where did it happen?"

"Her landlady, a Martha Green, gave the information. The doctor listed her death as consumption. The house is on Pratt Street."

Katherine glanced at Edith and Pat, out of earshot and doing a puzzle of Jeremy's.

"I've come from the house, and I spoke with Mrs. Green," the officer continued. "Seems Mrs. Tracy's friend left her a week before, and when Mrs. Green checked on Mrs. Tracy to try to collect the rent, she found her dead in bed and Pat gone. The doctor said she had only been dead for a day. He did ask around for the boy. When Mrs. Green checked on the contents in Pat's small room, it appeared he had taken one of the pillowslips, filling it with some of his clothes and possessions. He has simply become a lost child."

"Not anymore, Officer Pierce. My son, Jeremy, found him and brought him home to me. I thank you so much for your effort. Would you like to meet Pat?"

"Yes, ma'am, thank you. I don't want to frighten him."

"We will simply tell him you are Mr. Pierce, a friend of mine."

Pat was intent on the puzzle, and not too interested in the new face, although he politely said hello. Edith greeted the officer of the watch, sensing that something important had just taken place. Officer Pierce left for the Western Watch House. Katherine turned to Edith and asked if she could get a message to Richard and the two of them could join her and her family for supper tonight.

"What has happened, Katherine?" Edith asked impatiently, accepting the invitation for supper, and moving away from Pat.

"That was one of Mark's officers. He's been checking on Mary Tracy. She died last month of consumption,"

Katherine whispered. "According to their landlady, Pat simply ran away."

Edith's eyes filled with tears. "The poor child. He's been roaming around the city trying to fend for himself while looking for his mother or another woman to take her place."

"I know you like Pat, Edith. Would you consider giving him a home?"

Edith smiled broadly. "I would consider it very seriously."

"Do you think Richard might?"

"We'll find out at supper, won't we?"

Jamison had read about the Barnum robbery and murder, and wondered if Dr. Jones would also read about it. The doctor had seemed somewhat uneasy when asked about the soiled napkin Jamison would like returned. Now Dr. Jones knew where he was headed and had recommended a doctor in Ellicott's Mills. Would he start to tie things together and contact a policeman?

The artist was riding in the stagecoach with two other men and a woman. It was only a six mile trip to the railroad terminus in the mill town, then a few more miles to the Cliffside Inn in the country. From there how much longer would his destination be and would it be deeper in the country where transportation for him might be non-existent, and again would there be a full house? Most likely the Caton family would be staying elsewhere, not with their servants at the inn.

There was little conversation in the stagecoach, mostly talk about the weather, which was always a safe topic. The three men were all enjoying the bouncing effect of the stagecoach on the hilly turnpike that was causing the woman to almost spill out of her tightly laced bodice. Obviously the woman was not a lady, dressed in such a revealing manner. She was young, attractive, and seductive; used a fair amount of rouge and seemed to revel in the interest of the men. But she wasn't gaudy like a common prostitute. He would like to know her better. Jamison wondered where she was headed.

He might enjoy whatever she had to offer or sell. It might help to relieve his frustration.

He sat and brooded over his predicament. Safecracking required a careful, well thought out plan and it would be helpful to have an accomplice. If the Caton women had only stayed in Catonsville, he probably would have succeeded. But not to know where he was going except that it was in the country, and not to be sure there was a vehicle handy might mean long walking about an area unknown to him. If he arrived at the Cliffside Inn, was he going to ask the Cunningham girl where her mistress was? Not very likely. The servants would already be wondering why he was on their trail unless he could pretend to be lovesick over the lady's maid.

Jamison tried to put a value on the pearls. His money was running low. What should he do? As the stagecoach descended into the Patapsco Valley, he could see the terminus across the bridge. He made a quick decision. He would give up the pursuit of the jewelry, be satisfied with the black pearls, and get off here at the stop in Ellicott's Mills. If not too late, he could probably catch a locomotive that would take him the thirteen miles back to Baltimore. From there he could find transportation north and lose himself in New York. He was sure he could find a buyer there for his treasure.

Jamison was surprised to find that the woman was leaving the stagecoach with him at the terminus stop. He watched her walk over to the nearby hotel. She turned once and gave him a "come hither" smile. He continued on into the terminus with his baggage and leather case and found he was too late to make the trip to Baltimore today. He arranged for a ticket there early the next afternoon. He used a different name as he did fifteen minutes later when he registered at the hotel. The stone building had three floors and rose up right beside the river. He glanced at the name before him: Mrs. Sally Timmons.

"Mrs. Timmons and I were together on the stagecoach," he said to the clerk. "Could you please tell me her room number?"

The clerk sighed and said in a bored voice, "Second floor, room 210."

Jamison's room number was 214. "Is there an inexpensive place to eat close by?"

"We have a decent dining room, moderate in price. It will be open for supper in about an hour."

He went to his room, unpacked a few things, and washed up. The locked leather case went under the bed. He went outside and took a walk over the bridge, dodging traffic and quite fascinated by the intensity of the water coursing below the bridge. The railroad tracks were above him and the turnpike continued up the hill.

Jamison wondered what Mrs. Timmons was doing. If he wanted her for the night or at least part of it, he supposed an invitation to an inexpensive meal was a good start before she was claimed by someone else.

Robert Jamison, or William Rogers as he had signed the register at the Railway Hotel, returned to the premises and had a look at the dining room which seemed adequate for his purpose. He then went upstairs and knocked at the room numbered 210. After a moment or two, Mrs. Sally Timmons opened the door, and seemed to be expecting him. She had freshened up and put on a light low-cut gown. Her hair was combed in the latest sophisticated fashion and more rouge had been applied. There was no mistaking her profession, but he would enjoy some preliminary activity like a nice supper with wine before getting to the heart of the matter. It was still early in the evening.

She accepted his invitation to dine in a soft refined voice after he had introduced himself using his assumed name, and mentioned that he was in town on business with one of the mills. It was lonely traveling about and staying in hotels. She understood, didn't she? Sally understood very well. For the past five years, she had been catering to lonely men in nondescript hotels where her attractiveness outshone the surroundings. She also engaged in some petty larceny when the situation presented itself with the more affluent customers. She was gone from the hotel by the time the men discovered anything missing. She now considered herself a cunning expert, with a sizable bank account.

They both decided the evening looked promising.

Chapter 9   The Sister

Rocky was unceremoniously dropped on the ground when Joshua stood up from the bench to catch Becky in his arms.

"Oh, Becky, how I have missed you today," he sighed as he kissed her upturned mouth when she laid her head against his chest.

"No more than I have missed you, Joshua. I hoped to have seen you along the turnpike, but that didn't happen."

Rocky jumped back on the bench and sat staring disdainfully at the behavior of young love.

"How was your day, Becky?"

"Fairly good. I was glad when we came to the Manor. It's a very fine house. Quite large and set far back from the road. Foxes are about and deer, along with the farm animals. The family took the Baron and Baroness and her sisters and parents birdwatching, and then did some shooting late this afternoon."

"Do you have a nice room here?"

"Yes, and the dinner was good. Chicken and potatoes."

"I know. I had some. My room is in the attic, and Rocky is again in the stable."

"The ride in the stagecoach was terribly rough coming over the hills," Becky complained. "Was it a hard walk for you?"

Joshua smiled. "I've been a little out of breath most of the day, but I had some good sales. Rocky and I had lunch by the river in Ellicott's Mills, and I saw the terminus, and some locomotives, and such massive rocks."

"Yes, like being in the mountains. Not working in the kitchen here?"

"No, I helped feed the animals and tended to the horses. I will have to start back in the morning and return to Catonsville. By the time you arrive there the next day, I will be on the road home for shabbes," he said sadly.

Becky took his hand in hers, and looked intently into his eyes. "Do you like this life, Joshua?"

"I've gained a lot of respect for my fellow peddlers. How anyone makes it round trip from Baltimore to Frederick and back in five days is hard to believe. I've been lucky with the weather so far; nice, warm, sunny days. It is harder work than I expected. To tell you the truth, Becky, peddling only makes me want to drive locomotives more than anything else in the world."

"We have locomotives in England. Why don't you return with us? Then we could be together," she ventured boldly.

"What are you saying, Becky?"

"If you can't get the job you want here, you might be able to in England, and the countryside is so very beautiful."

"But I have my family in Baltimore, and where could I get money for the fare to cross the ocean?"

"Maybe the Baron could work something out with you." Becky wanted Joshua. She was certain he wanted her. Tonight was not going to be the end of their relationship if she could help it.

"Becky, this is only the third evening we've spent together. Do you think…?"

"Joshua, do you want us to be like ships passing in the night? If so, we'll say goodnight now." She lowered her head and folded her hands in her lap, waiting for the response she wanted. There was no comment from Joshua. Hurt and embarrassed, she stood up, and kissed him on the cheek. Still no response. She turned and went inside the back door of the hotel where she waited for him to follow. He didn't come in. She waited a few more moments, then went into the lobby where she saw Lt. Bennett and Officer Cavanaugh checking in.

"Miss Cunningham, good evening," said the lieutenant with a tired smile. "I'm glad to see you arrived safely. Have you by any chance seen Mr. Jamison, the artist?"

"No, sir," she answered. "Why would he be here?"

"We had been told at the Piedmont Hotel in Catonsville that he had booked a room here for at least tonight. He doesn't seem to have arrived."

"The other servants and myself have been here since before supper. I don't think we have seen him since Catonsville." Becky looked puzzled. "Could he have wanted to sketch the Manor? It's a very impressive house, but I saw him nowhere on the grounds."

"Seems he changed his mind," growled Officer Cavanaugh, "but we're here for the night."

"In case you do see him anywhere, Miss Cunningham, I have to advise you to keep your distance and inform the Baron. We believe he may be the suspect we are looking for in the theft of the pearls and the murder of the man at Barnum's Hotel," Bennett said quietly, as Becky's hand flew to her mouth while she turned as pale as the moon.

"He's following us, isn't he? Does he think we have more jewelry with us for him to steal? We don't, you know. It's at …"

"Don't say anymore, please. People are about. This is a public room," warned Bennett. "Come. Shall we sit on the porch for a while?" They went outside and moved to a corner where there was some privacy. Guests were returning to their bedrooms.

"Maybe he has gone farther west, Lt. Bennett," Becky suggested, "although I have been told there isn't much between here and Frederick and that is still a long way."

"He should be seeing a doctor for his hand tomorrow. Jamison has been given the name of one in Ellicott's Mills. He could have seen the futility of his plan and is backing off."

"He could catch the locomotive from Ellicott's Mills to Baltimore and lose himself in the city, or head north to Philadelphia or New York," Cavanaugh reasoned.

"Good point," Bennett added wearily. "In the morning we will return to Ellicott's Mills; check the doctor, and the locomotive schedule for today and tomorrow to Baltimore. He might have been able to catch one today. I might as well call on the Baroness while we are here in the morning to bring her up to date on the case."

"So I shall see you in the morning at the hotel or the Manor, sir?" asked Becky, anxious to tell Joshua the news about the artist who was a suspect.

"God willing, Miss Cunningham. Try to sleep well."

Bennett and Cavanaugh went to the kitchen to see what might still be available in the way of a late supper, although the dining room was now closed.

Becky went out back looking for Joshua and his cat, but they were no longer there. She went to bed and cried herself to sleep.

Jeremy ended up taking a message to Richard about supper when he returned from school. Katherine sent the boy to a bakery to pick up some dessert to enhance her supper. She wished Lexington Market was open, but she would have to make do with the amount of ham and vegetables she had planned on. She and Jeremy would eat sparingly.

Edith helped her in the basement kitchen while Jeremy played a game with Pat.

"The boys seem to be getting along," Edith commented.

"Jeremy is getting used to having Pat around, but he still is a bit leery and calls him a pickpocket," Katherine smiled.

Edith was nervous as she set the table. "Oh, I can't wait for Richard to come and see him. When will Mark be home?"

"It should be soon." Katherine glanced at the shelf clock, certain that any minute her husband would be walking through the door.

Edith said, "I think Pat might be the answer to a prayer. Maybe you would let him spend the night with us so we could have a longer visit."

Before Katherine could answer, they heard a knock upstairs, and heavy footsteps heading their way. "I'm here," called Richard. "Has Mark come home?"

"Not yet. Come down and meet our guest," Katherine responded.

The gregarious Richard came down, kissed the two women, shook hands with Jeremy, and extended his hand to a smiling Pat.

Edith took Richard by the arm and made him go back upstairs where in twenty minutes she explained Pat's presence and her hopes. A more sedate Richard returned to the kitchen and asked Katherine for a pint of beer.

Katherine and Edith finished preparations while Richard watched the two boys at their game. Katherine wondered why Mark wasn't home yet.

"The food is ready. We will have to begin without Mark," she announced anxiously. She placed Pat between Edith and Richard who tried to make small talk with the boy. Pat conversed shyly and was mannerly at the table. Everyone but Jeremy seemed a little nervous, then Katherine was jolted by a knock on the front door, upstairs.

Excusing herself, she went up and found Officer Pierce on her doorstep again. He noticed the fear in her face.

"Not to worry, Mrs. Bennett. I have a message for you that came by stagecoach to the Watch House a short time ago. Lt. Bennett is delayed near Ellicott's Mills for the night. Everything is fine, but he wanted you to know about the delay."

Katherine took the note with trembling hands and tore it open. She had not been alone without Mark since they were married. After reading it, and feeling relieved, she thanked Officer Pierce.

"One more thing I have to tell you, ma'am. A woman came into the Watch House after having seen Pat Tracy's sketch in the newspaper. She knows the boy, used to live next door some time ago. She says Pat's sister is living with her and wanted to know what she should tell the girl about her mother. Perhaps you might want to visit her. Here is her name and address. The boy never mentioned a sister, did he?"

"No," said Katherine, barely able to speak. "He never did."

Katherine thanked the officer again for bringing her the message. "I will visit Mrs. Martin and try to sort this out." She closed the door behind Officer Pierce and slowly walked to the basement steps. Questions flew through her mind. Why hadn't Pat mentioned his sister? Did he even know her? She might as well question the boy with the others present, but she would wait until after supper, and only tell them about Mark's delay.

"I am sorry for the interruption," Katherine said as she returned to the kitchen. "An officer of the watch brought me a message from Mark. Seems he has to stay overnight in Ellicott's Mills with Officer Cavanaugh in pursuit of a suspect in the Barnum's Hotel robbery and murder case."

"Gee, I wish I was there," Jeremy exclaimed. "I could be a big help."

"You can be a big help here, being the man of the house," Katherine replied. "You will protect us through the night."

"That does sound exciting for Mark," Edith said with enthusiasm. "I suppose it could be very dangerous."

"Don't upset Katherine," Richard admonished. "Ellicott's Mills. That town has become very industrialized with all the mills along the Patapsco River. Really increased the railroad traffic with shipping freight to Baltimore."

"What kind of mills are there, Richard?" Edith asked.

"Used to be mostly tobacco farmers there, but the Ellicott brothers came in and soon wheat replaced tobacco. The town is full of flour mills, paper mills, grist mills, textile mills, saw mills, not to mention quarrying granite, and the iron works. That's just a sample. Quite a bustling place."

"Doesn't sound like a very nice place to live," Katherine decided, "although I suppose there is enough employment for everyone."

"Unfortunately there are child labor problems. Young children are used particularly in the cotton mills tending the looms. Some are so small they are put on stools or chairs to reach their work. Most of the children work ten hours a day, and many accidents occur. There is a desperate need for reform."

"Let us talk about something pleasant, Richard," Edith insisted. "Katherine, may I help you serve dessert?"

"You know that is one of my favorite subjects," Richard laughed, patting his round stomach. "Are we having cake or pie?"

"Cherry tarts," Katherine replied. "They look very good. The tarts are from the bakery." Hopefully they would also sweeten his mood for the coming news.

After dessert and tea, Katherine brought up the subject of Pat and his sister. In a shaky voice she asked Pat the name of his sister. He didn't answer.

"Sister?" said a surprised Edith and Richard in unison.

"Officer Pierce also told me a little while ago that a woman came to the Watch House having recognized Pat's sketch in the paper. She told him she knew Pat as a next door neighbor and that Pat's sister was living with her."

"Why have you not mentioned her, Pat?" asked Richard. The authoritative voice made an impression on the boy. He decided he should answer the question.

"I forgot where she is. Abby is her name."

"How old is she?"

"If I am six or seven, then she is eight or nine, I think."

"Why was she not living with you and your mother?" Richard continued.

"Abby had to go to work. It is not my time yet."

Katherine was glad Richard had taken over the questioning. She thought she was about ready to break down and cry. Even Richard's voice faltered as he asked Pat a final question.

"When was the last time you saw Abby?"

"I don't remember. Maybe it was Easter. Ma and me took her some candy."

Everyone fell silent. Pat asked if he could be excused. Katherine said yes, and Jeremy offered to play another game upstairs with him. After the boys left the room, Katherine thanked Edith and Richard for their help.

"I intend to visit Mrs. Martin and Abby tomorrow. Mrs. Martin is concerned about telling Abby about her mother, and wants to know what the girl's situation is, working for her."

"The children are orphans. The court will have to decide who will take charge of them. Are there any living relatives? Perhaps Mrs. Martin knows. The immediate problem is where they will stay until the court decides." Richard turned to a tearful Edith. "I know nothing of this procedure, but I will find out as soon as I can. Edith, you go with Katherine to visit Abby and Mrs. Martin and we will see what we can do to help. I can't make you any promises at this time, but we will help in some way."

Chapter 10   The Prostitute

All through dinner, Robert Jamison, alias William Rogers, and Sally Timmons lied to each other about almost everything. He lied about his name, she lied about her place of origin. They both lied about their marital status and families and life experiences. Only Sally didn't misrepresent her profession. She considered herself a very good prostitute, almost artistic. She could offer him almost anything that suited his tastes.

They dined on good beefsteak, roasted potatoes, and early peas. A choice red wine accompanied the meal, and hot tea and chocolate cake finished it off. They were very relaxed having consumed a bottle of wine between them. Lingering over the tea, and in no rush to leave the dining room, they began to form opinions about each other.

In the stagecoach, Sally had noticed the black leather case that the man held tightly on his lap. She was curious to know what it contained. The man himself was well dressed and polite. He had been generous to invite her for supper, and treat her with some respect, knowing her profession. Not a quick hour in the hotel room, like most men, and goodbye. Sally liked the added attention.

Jamison truly enjoyed her company. He found her to be refined, pretty and personable. He also liked her sense of humor. He began thinking again of another accomplice. She might do very well. They could join up and take off for a new adventure in New York.

It was growing dark, and Sally suggested a walk along the bridge under the lanterns and the moon to view the river coursing by the town. Once on the bridge, they looked back to the hotel and were amazed at how close it came to the river's edge. With the open windows in the rooms, one would hear the lapping along the banks and the hissing water. The wind was beginning to pick up and they headed back to the hotel. Sally asked him about his hand injury and he told her it was a dog bite.

"How about spending the entire night with me, Sally?"

"I suppose I will have to make an adjustment in my fee for the delicious supper," she laughed.

"I don't require constant entertainment. There will be time to sleep and rest."

"Would you like to come to my room?"

"Yes, that's good." He didn't want her near his baggage or leather case. "Is it going to cost me a fortune to have you all night?" he smiled.

"I can't tell you exactly what it will be. You see, it's rather like a menu. The price depends on what specialty you want to order, and the actual time involved." She said it with a merry look in her eye, and he burst out laughing.

"Sally, I think you and I could get along very well. Are you only staying here one night?"

"No, it's a long way to come from Baltimore for one night."

"I could stay another day, maybe. He took her arm and they proceeded up to the second floor. "I may be in a position to offer you a partnership in a more lucrative profession," Jamison said.

"Is it legitimate?" Sally gave him a sly look.

Being very close to her, he was beginning to feel aroused. "We can discuss that at breakfast. Let's go to bed."

Sally Timmons proved spectacular in bed. It wasn't easy to make love with one sore hand in a bandage, but she made him comfortable, and was worth whatever she would demand from him in the morning. Throughout the night, there were long periods of sleep, and when she thought he was in a particularly deep slumber near dawn, she slipped from the bed and put on a voluminous robe. She snatched his keys from the bureau near his money clip and coin purse, and silently left the room.

An hour later, he slowly awoke and reached for her in bed. Where was she? Could she have gone to one of the privies in the back of the hotel? He fell asleep again, then suddenly sat up in bed fully awake. Glancing at the bureau he saw his money clip and coin purse, but where were his keys? Quickly he partially dressed, then went outside the room and moved along the hall to his room. The door was locked. He knocked quietly. She didn't answer, although he thought he heard a movement inside. He knocked again louder, and a sleepy voice came through the door.

"Who is there?"

"Sally, it's me, William. Why are you in there?"

She opened the door slowly, staying by the threshold as he crossed over.

"Where is the key to my room?" she asked.

"I left the door open. The key is inside in the lock." He looked around the room and everything seemed in place; his baggage and leather case, and the bed was rumpled.

"You were restless, and snoring, and I was having trouble sleeping. I decided to go to bed in your room," Sally sighed, pushing her hair away from her face. "Do you mind?"

Jamison wanted to believe her, but she had taken the key to the leather case. "You only needed to take the door key. Why did you take the small key?"

"They were together. I simply picked them both up in the dark."

It was plausible. The two keys were together on the table side by side. He wanted the story to be true. He was truly fond of the woman, but he had to know.

"Go on back to your room, Sally," he said in a tired voice. "I'm going to wash and dress, and you tell me what I owe you. Will you come to breakfast with me?"

Jamison noticed the relief in her eyes, as she stepped into the hall. "Come to my room when you are ready," she answered.

He closed the door behind her and pulled his leather case to the bed. He opened the case and looked for the black pearls in the napkin. They were gone, and so was Sally, back to her locked room.

Jamison couldn't believe it. Not only a prostitute, but also a thief! How could he accuse her? She probably knew

80

about the robbery and murder at Barnum's. She had come on the stagecoach from Baltimore and certainly heard the news or read about it. He had to get the pearls back. He could act as though he didn't know about the theft. That would be the only way he could get back in her room where he could forcibly search her and her baggage behind a locked door. He washed and dressed, then went to her room supposedly to settle his account before taking her down to breakfast. He had also left some clothes in her room.

Sally knew he would check the leather case and find the pearls missing. He would be stupid if he didn't. She must never be alone with him again. Having read the newspaper article, and now realizing he must be the culprit, there was a possibility that the next murder victim might be her. Two choices occurred to the prostitute and that was selling the pearls in New York, or giving them back to Baroness Stafford to collect a reward. Packed and dressed in a more sensible, modest traveling outfit, she wanted to leave the hotel immediately, and not be trapped here like a rat.

There was a knock on the door. She didn't answer, hoping he might think she left. He knocked again.

"Are you ready, Sally?"

She replied through the door. "Would you do me a favor, please? Have your breakfast downstairs in the dining room, and ask the waiter to send me up a tray, just tea and toast. I'm still packing."

Jamison knew they were playing a cat and mouse game. Was she prepared to stay in the room all day or until the maid came to make it up? How could he flush her out? He needed to see the doctor and catch his locomotive. He would try a different approach.

"You can get your own breakfast, Sally. I told you I would settle up with you. How much do you want?"

"Ten dollars. Please slip it under the door."

"And will you return my property that you took from my case this morning?" he asked in a low, nasty voice.

"I took nothing that belongs to you, and you have your money clip and change purse that you left in my room, and it is intact. Leave the ten dollars and that will be the end of it. Goodbye, William." She had no intention of returning the few clothes left in her room.

"No goodbyes yet. When you leave the room, I will be waiting for you."

Nothing to do but create a diversion, thought the prostitute. Sally was fully dressed, and packed. The pearls were still wrapped in the napkin and tucked in her purse.

Suddenly she opened the door and came out screaming, holding all her possessions. Jamison was startled by her outburst and tried to grab her, but by now other bedroom doors were opening and two men were coming to her rescue.

"Help me, please help me," she cried. "That man is trying to attack me. He wants to rob me." She ran screaming to the stairs, then down to the lobby.

The men tried to restrain Jamison, but were no match for the larger man. He pushed them both out of his way, then retreated to his room to collect his baggage and case. When he got down to the lobby, the manager was threatening to call a policeman and demanding payment of his bill. Jamison told the manager that the woman was his estranged wife, and he was at the hotel trying to bring about a reconciliation. Didn't he remember that they arrived on the same stagecoach, even though they registered under different names?

The manager wasn't interested in a long drawn out story. He just wanted peace and quiet in the hotel. Jamison continued his sad tale. The dining room help would have seen them cordially having supper together last night. Unfortunately this morning, his wife had gone slightly berserk, and wanted no part of him. As Jamison profusely apologized for the woman's behavior, the manger, himself caught in an unhappy marriage, told him with a deep sigh to pay his bill, and quietly leave the premises.

Meanwhile, Sally, having previously taken care of her account, crossed over the bridge to the terminus and bought a ticket for Baltimore. When Jamison appeared later in the terminus, he saw her quietly having breakfast in an adjoining café surrounded by other hungry travelers. Checking on her destination with the booking clerk, he found she would be on the same locomotive. Suddenly realizing that he was famished, Jamison shared a table with some other passengers and satisfied his hunger.

Several hours were left before the locomotive would arrive from the west, and take on new passengers. He would check his baggage and leather case, now only containing the safecracking tools, and walk up the hill to find the doctor. The throbbing in his hand was increasing and there also seemed to be some swelling.

Sally watched him leave the terminus and suspected he was off to see the doctor. It ran through her mind that she could exchange her ticket for Frederick, but she felt that the very best decision would be to go straight to the Western Watch House in Baltimore. A Lt. Bennett was listed in the article as being in charge of the case. Returning the pearls to the rightful owner must certainly earn her a reward. Identifying the thief would qualify her for police protection until the culprit was apprehended. The important way to stay safe until this took place was to surround herself with people until she arrived in Baltimore.

Jamison returned to the terminus with a scowl on his face. The doctor had given him a discouraging report. The infection was worse; the hand swollen and red. The doctor treated it as best he could with alcohol and noticed that the patient had a slight fever. Dr. Miller advised Jamison to enter a hospital as soon as he reached Baltimore.

Sally was seated in a corner of the waiting lounge, reading a romance novel. Jamison sat across from her, glaring, then opened a newspaper that had just arrived on an early westbound stagecoach. Each watched the other surreptitiously, aware of any movement of the other as they pretended to read.

An hour later, the station master who was visibly agitated, made an announcement. All the locomotives were cancelled for today because of a huge rockslide on the tracks.

83

Ticket holders could obtain a refund or exchange their tickets for tomorrow when, hopefully, the railroad tracks would be cleared. If they needed immediate transportation, they could try at the Railroad Hotel to book a stagecoach seat for Baltimore today, or find overnight accommodations.

Sally and Jamison exchanged a brief, angry look; both deciding to dispense with the refund until they had secured stagecoach seats. Gathering up their belongings, they hurriedly recrossed the bridge to the Railroad Hotel where they fell in line with other disgruntled travelers while Sally tried to keep her distance from Jamison.

Chapter 11 Becky in Pursuit

The Patapsco, an Algonquian Indian name, is a formidable river fifty-two miles long. Beginning in the center of Maryland in a spring-fed farm pond, it carves a twisting rock-strewn path, and finally empties into the Chesapeake Bay. On its shores, early Indian settlements flourished while food gatherers fished the waters. Historical events occurred in the vicinity of the Patapsco along with commerce and industrialization. Tobacco moved east, at last giving way to wheat, and the young railroad moved west.

The Patapsco slides between high granite boulders and deep forests. The river can be benign or threatening. It is never still; always in constant motion. Each heavy rainfall is a cause for concern.

Early Thursday morning, Joshua left a note for Miss Becky Cunningham with the manager of the Cliffside Inn. He put on his peddler's coat and slipped on his backpack, both only half full, for the return trip to Baltimore and home. With a good breakfast under his belt, and his cat, Rocky, beside him, he glanced at the sky and thought again how lucky he had been not to have encountered any rain for the first half of the week.

Only his heart was heavy. He knew he would never see Becky again, and he hated to leave their short relationship in such shambles. He did care for her very much, but he had nothing to offer her and they were both so very young.

It was too early and the houses too sparse to begin peddling, so he concentrated on making good time getting to Ellicott's Mills. He looked down to see if Rocky was keeping up with him, but the cat had decided to sit down in the middle of the road a good way back, with his head turned in the direction of the inn. Joshua called to the animal who ignored him and started licking his paws.

"Come on, Rocky! You won't last long sitting there like you own the road." Joshua continued on, hoping the cat would soon follow. Stopping and looking behind him once more, the peddler noticed that Rocky hadn't moved, but when he saw Joshua's face, he let out a low mournful cry. Joshua sighed deeply, turned back and scooped up his cat. "She's not coming with us, you stupid animal." He hugged Rocky to him. "It's you and me. Learn now, cat, that you can't have everything you want in life."

Becky received the note from the manager an hour after Joshua had left the hotel. Waiting with the personal servants on the porch for the carriage to take them to the Manor, Becky retreated to a far corner and with her back to the others, tore open the envelope.

My very dear Becky,

I am so very sorry for the way last evening ended. Please try to understand that I do care for you, but I have nothing in this world to offer you. I can barely take care of myself. You are so fortunate to have your position with Baroness Stafford. You have the opportunity to travel, and be in beautiful houses.

Someday when you are older, you will meet the one who can give you what you deserve in life. For now, I have to try to make my way in the world. Always remember our short, mostly happy time together.

Joshua

Becky welled up with emotion, unaware that the carriage was ready to leave with the others on board.

"Come along, Becky," Mr. Ridley insisted. "Doesn't do to be late."

The lady's maid put the note back in the envelope, then tucked it in her pocket. She took out her handkerchief and blew her nose. Becky lowered her head to hide her teary eyes as she stepped into the carriage. The Baroness would help her; she would understand.

It was the middle of the morning and Lady Stafford thought young Becky had caught a cold. There was much sniffing and coughing from her maid as they sorted through the clean linens and clothing. Becky was trying to decide how to present her dilemma to her lady. After all, her employer had told her to come to her any time she had a problem. And every minute, Joshua was getting farther away from her. As Becky carried some lingerie to a bureau drawer, she suddenly burst into tears. With raised eyebrows, Lady Stafford asked Becky not to cry all over her clean underclothes.

"I'm sorry, my lady, but I have a terrible problem, and you did say I might come to you as if you were my mother."

"Yes, that is true, my dear. Sit down and tell me your troubles." The Baroness took the bundle of laundry from Becky and put it away in a drawer.

"It's like this. I met a Jewish peddler at the Piedmont Hotel, and then he was again at the Cliffside Inn and we've become friends, and now we have had to separate, and I think I'm in love." Becky choked on her story, and looked devastated.

The Baroness had to sit down to better comprehend what she was being told. "A Jewish peddler?" She too had a vision of an older man with a long beard.

"Oh, my lady, he is a very young peddler, only twenty and quite nice looking. I think he loves me." Becky reached into her pocket and withdrew the note, handing it to the Baroness. Lady Stafford slowly read the note while Becky sat and sobbed.

"Becky, you and Joshua haven't done anything illicit, have you?"

"Certainly not, my lady. Only some kissing and cuddling."

"Your Joshua sounds like a level-headed young man. Does he enjoy being a peddler?"

"No, my lady. He wants to be a locomotive driver, but there are too many applicants to the Baltimore and Ohio Railroad."

The Baroness was quite familiar with the railroad. "My grandfather was very involved with its establishment toward the end of his life. For many years, my sisters and I have been away from our country, but my father, Mr. Caton, has always lived here since before his marriage. He had some part in assisting my grandfather in the venture. He probably knows of someone at the Baltimore and Ohio who might help Joshua find a job."

Becky stopped sobbing and dabbed at her eyes with her handkerchief. "But Joshua is probably in Ellicott's Mills already. I don't know where he lives with his family in Baltimore."

Lady Stafford smiled at Becky, a bit of mischief in her expression.

"Of course, I would like to meet him first before I could recommend him. Shall we order up the carriage and go to Ellicott's Mills?"

"You would do that for me, your maid?" asked Becky, her eyes as wide as saucers.

"I want you to be happy and if you think chasing him down will help solve the problem, I'm ready to go."

Becky couldn't resist embracing her mistress.

"The heartbreak of a romance gone awry for a young girl of eighteen can last a lifetime," the Baroness said sadly. "I know. That is one reason I waited so long to marry. Waited so long that like my two noble sisters, I probably won't have children of my own."

She took Becky's hand. "When I selected you to be my maid, it was because you were young and seemed to be someone I might mother a bit, so here is more advice. We must be somewhat business-like, my dear. You mustn't simply throw yourself at Joshua. We are going to ask him if he would be interested in my effort to pursue a job for him at the railroad."

"Yes, my lady. I see that would be the right course to take. Am I interrupting any of your plans for today?"

"Not this morning. We shouldn't be gone very long. You tidy yourself up. I will tell the Baron we are on a shopping errand, and he will see to the carriage. One word of caution, Becky. Not a word to my sisters, or we will end up being a foursome."

As Becky and the Baroness pulled away from the Manor house on their mission, Lt. Bennett and Officer Cavanaugh came through the gate in their carriage. Recognizing Lady Stafford and Miss Cunningham, Bennett signaled to them to stop.

"Oh, I forgot," Becky said regretfully, "to tell you, my lady, that I saw Lt. Bennett last night at the Cliffside Inn and he was coming to call today."

"Good morning, Lady Stafford, and Miss Cunningham. May I have a few minutes of your time?"

The two women had no choice but to let the lieutenant join them in their carriage.

"I wanted to bring you up to date on the case," explained Bennett as Officer Cavanaugh waited in their carriage.

"That is very kind of you to come all the way here to give us whatever information you have," murmured the Baroness.

"We are also in pursuit of the suspect, Robert Jamison, the artist. In Catonsville we found he had stayed at the Piedmont Hotel and visited a Dr. Jones who treated his hand. Fortunately the doctor saved some evidence; a Barnum's napkin with a piece of a champagne bottle wrapped inside. The doctor also told us he was heading to Ellicott's Mills and needed the name of a doctor there. It is quite evident that Jamison is following your entourage from place to place to attempt another robbery."

"But we left all the jewelry at Castle Thunder," Lady Stafford protested.

"Jamison thinks you are carrying it with you. He had ordered a room at the Cliffside Inn, but for some reason we think he changed his mind and left the stagecoach in Ellicott's Mills. We had thought to apprehend him at the inn last night, but we are returning to see if after visiting the doctor, he may be trying to return to Baltimore with only the

89

pearls. Once he arrives back in Baltimore, he could go on to New York or Philadelphia."

"Why has he decided not to pursue us?" asked the Baroness.

"I don't think he expected you to be traveling around so much, and with so many people," answered the lieutenant. "It takes time to plan a robbery, assess the layout of the place, and the movements of the people. In less than a week, you have been at Barnum's Hotel, Castle Thunder, and here at the Manor."

"His hand injury must also be an obstacle," Becky said.

"Yes. The hand has to be treated daily, and there is pain. Also, he is easily identified by the bandage. We had better find him before he boards that locomotive." Bennett apologized for keeping them from wherever they were going.

"Becky and I are on a shopping errand to Ellicott's Mills, so you may want to ride ahead or behind, but I do thank you for taking the time to inform us, and I hope you will catch him today."

On their way again, the Baroness decided it might be helpful to know of Becky's experience with the opposite sex. How serious was this three night romance? Becky had only been with her for a year, and Lady Stafford had tried to afford her some sort of private life, which wasn't much with their close proximity to each other. An eighteen year old girl had shown her mistress her intensity, and a twenty year old boy, who was scarcely a man, had written a very mature note, and thought seriously of the future. Did they have any future?

"Becky, have you had any romantic entanglements before?"

"Since I was fifteen, some young men have shown an interest, and I have been courted once or twice, but I never felt about them the way I do about Joshua. If I lose him, I will never be the same again."

Lady Stafford knew what she was feeling. "I'll help you as much as I can, my dear."

They were at the top of the hill heading through the town toward the river. Lt. Bennett and Office Cavanaugh were behind them. The carriage slowed so Becky could search both sides of the road for Joshua, irritating a long line of vehicles in the rear, including the police. Lady Stafford sat back and enjoyed looking out at the shops, houses and people along the busy road.

Midway, Becky glanced out the back window and saw the lieutenant's carriage stop at a house with Dr. Miller's sign. As she turned to continue her search, she saw Rocky stretched out on the walkway in front of a house. Joshua must be inside.

"Stop, please," she called, tapping a cane on the partition separating the driver from the passengers. The carriage stopped abruptly, almost causing a collision. "There's Rocky!"

Lady Stafford looked out the window and saw an elegant tabby sunning himself.

"Who is Rocky?"

"Joshua's cat, my lady. Joshua is peddling at that house!"

In Dr. Miller's office the policemen had a brief chat with the doctor concerning his patient with the injured hand.

"Yes, Mr. William Rogers was in earlier this morning. He was referred to me by Dr. Jones in Catonsville. He's feverish with a badly infected hand that is quite swollen and red. I treated it as Dr. Jones had with alcohol, and put on a clean bandage. I did advise Mr. Rogers to get to a hospital at once when he reached Baltimore."

"Today?" Bennett asked quickly. "Today he was going to Baltimore?"

"Yes, by locomotive."

"Do you know what time it leaves?"

"Soon, in an hour or so."

Other than to thank Dr. Miller, Bennett and Cavanaugh wasted not one more moment. Hurriedly they left the office, and went down the hill as fast as possible in the carriage to the terminus. There they were told about the cancellation of today's locomotives due to the rockslide. Mr. Rogers could be trying to make a stagecoach connection to Baltimore, they were told, since he had not approached the booking clerk yet about his locomotive ticket. The two policemen were directed to the Railroad Hotel.

Chapter 12   The Town of Oella

With Pat in tow, Katherine and Edith called upon Mrs. Martin on Thursday morning. The house was very modest on Fayette Street, and the woman was kind, but harried. There was an odor present reflecting that too many people were living in cramped quarters. Mrs. Martin recognized Pat at once, and hugged him. She politely invited her guests to take seats in the parlor among the clutter.

"I believe Officer Pierce told you I might call," Katherine began. "I am his superior's wife, Mrs. Bennett, and this is my sister-in-law, Mrs. Coughlin."

"Let me find Abby. She will be so happy to see Pat."

"Please wait, Mrs. Martin," Katherine continued. "Could you first give us some information on Mary Tracy, her husband, and the circumstances that have brought us here?"

Mrs. Martin wiped her hands on her apron and sat across from her guests with her arm around Pat.

"Mr. Tracy died a few years ago and Mary has had a very hard time trying to support her children; mostly handouts from friends, in and out of almshouses, unable to work because of her consumption. She brought Abby to me to take her on as nursemaid and housemaid in return for her keep, clothing and necessities. Mary and Pat visited occasionally, but I understand from Officer Pierce her condition worsened and when she died, Pat ran away."

"Yes, my son, Jeremy, brought him home from off the street. He's been with us for the past few days while we have tried to identify him." Katherine glanced at Pat when his mother's death was mentioned, the first time he had heard it, but there was no response.

"We are very grateful you came forward about the sketch in the paper."

"I'm glad he has been in such very good care. I haven't told Abby yet. Shall I bring her down? She's upstairs with some of the children."

Katherine said yes, and wondered how many children Abby was caring for.

"I think it best if you would tell her about her mother alone since she knows you so well."

Fifteen minutes later, Abby came down the steps with a two and a three year old. More childish noise was ringing through the upstairs rooms. Abby was small and thin. She had similar features as Pat and the same blonde hair and blue eyes. She was crying, but managed a slight smile when she saw her brother. Pat ran to her and grabbed her around her waist.

Mrs. Martin introduced the pretty girl to the adults.

"How old are you, Abby?" Katherine asked kindly.

"I believe I am nine," she replied. "I thought my mother might be dead. It's a long time since she visited and she was so very sick at Easter." Such a very grownup comment, thought Katherine.

"Mrs. Bennett needs to talk to you about where you and Pat should be staying until things are sorted out with your mother's passing," Mrs. Martin explained. "Pat is staying with her for a while."

"The question seems to be, Abby," Katherine went on, hoping the word orphanage would not crop up in the conversation, "whom would you like to be with at this time?"

Without hesitation and a careful glance at Mrs. Martin, Abby answered, "I want to be with Pat. We need to be together. I would also like to be able to go to school."

Edith asked, "Have you ever been in school?"

"No, but Mrs. Martin has taught me some reading when the children are in bed."

"We haven't much time for teaching as you can see. Our hands are full," Mrs. Martin replied with embarrassment.

"When would you like to leave, Abby? Perhaps tomorrow?" Edith wanted to know. "You do need to pack and give Mrs. Martin some notice."

The child's eyes filled again with tears. "I haven't very much to pack. I only need about fifteen minutes to put my things in a bag." She turned to her employer. "How much longer do you want me to stay?"

"Oh, you can leave now, child. You know I will miss you and so will the children, but of course, you want to be with your brother."

Abby looked relieved. She wanted very much to be rescued from the heavy work load.

"Mrs. Martin, did you have any sort of written agreement with Mary Tracy about Abby being here?" Katherine asked.

"No," the woman answered with a trace of irritation. "We were neighbors. I wanted to help Mary, and this is what she suggested. It was a friendly agreement."

Katherine was suspicious that Abby was getting the short end of the stick. "How many children do you have, Mrs. Martin?"

"Five," she answered cautiously.

"What are their ages?"

"All under six," she replied lamely. "And when are you due, Mrs. Bennett?" Mrs. Martin wanted to change the subject. She didn't want to be reported as overworking Abby.

"In a few week's time. Well, Abby, if Mrs. Martin has no objections, why don't you get your things together and we will leave."

Abby didn't need to be told twice. She flew up the stairs, packed, kissed each of the children goodbye, among much wailing, and politely bid Mrs. Martin goodbye.

Outside in the fresh air, Abby took a deep breath, and holding Pat's hand, went with the ladies who told her they were going to have lunch at a nice eatery.

Katherine worried all through lunch what Mark would say when he returned home today to find Pat still there and also Abby. She simply did not have the room, or the energy. Edith must help her for a short time by taking them in, while Richard did whatever he could. Was it too much to ask them for a temporary home for the children?

Edith thought Katherine looked exhausted. They took a carriage to Katherine's house, and Edith insisted on being given Pat's clothes. "Pat and Abby will spend a few nights with us until Richard finds a solution. You lie down and take a nap."

Katherine thanked Edith with a deep sigh and kissed both children goodbye.

At the Railroad Hotel, Sally Timmons and Robert Jamison, alias William Rogers, were able to secure stagecoach seats for the afternoon trip to Baltimore. Separately, they both checked their baggage, and Jamison his leather case, at the hotel to be placed on the stagecoach prior to departure. Sally immediately returned to the terminus booking clerk to collect her refund on today's cancelled locomotive. She was surprised that William had not done the same. In fact, she had lost track of him.

From walking about in the warmth of the June day, Jamison was thirsty and wanted to find a cool place to rest for the next few hours before leaving Ellicott's Mills. He had gotten a large glass of water from the hotel, then remembered seeing from the terminus a nice shady area across the bridge on the river bank. It was a small mill town called Oella where many of the mill workers lived. There were long brick rows of small houses, and single houses hastily and poorly put together. Scattered over the hills were treacherous dirt roads linking the dwellings. Near some leafy willow trees, which dipped toward the river, stood a small more carefully constructed chapel of stone and wood. He felt it would be someplace to rest that would be cool and private. With his water glass in hand, he crossed the bridge and entered Oella. He walked a few minutes more observing the river, then turned toward the chapel and reached for the handle on the door finding it unlocked.

Most of the people in the town would be at work at the mills. He saw no one and no one saw him. He entered the one room chapel, a soft light coming through one modest stained glass window depicting the Good Shepherd. There had been no sign outside and there was no indication inside of the denomination of the chapel. There was an altar and a simple wooden cross and some candles. Rows of wooden pews with cushions beckoned to him.

He was sweating profusely, and his hand was throbbing more than ever. He felt absolutely exhausted. He removed his jacket and opened his shirt collar. Rolling up the jacket, he put it in one of the pews like a pillow, removed his shoes and reclined full length in the pew to take a nap. Since it was a weekday, he hoped no one would venture in. If he could only rest for an hour or so, he could stand the long trip to Baltimore by stagecoach.

At first he fretted about Sally and the retrieval of the pearls. He had to keep up his strength to get them back. How long was it going to take to get her alone somewhere? Dr. Miller had told him to go directly to a hospital when he reached Baltimore. Did many people die from infections? What a mess this had turned out to be. He was responsible for one man's death, and he was afraid that in his frustration, if she maddened him enough, he might kill Sally. Women had always been trouble for him. He thought Sally was different and they might form a partnership. That plan had been dashed. His throat was parched and he sat up in the pew and finished off the glass of water. He swayed slightly with dizziness, and reclined again on the cushions. He had to sleep. He fell into a deep slumber as the willows outside swept along the bank and the river surged.

Sally Timmons was sitting in the Railroad Hotel lobby killing time by reading her romance novel until the stagecoach was due to leave for Baltimore. She kept watching the door for William Rogers, and heard his name mentioned at the desk when two men came in to speak with the manager. After a few minutes, the manager nodded in her direction informing the men that the woman sitting there was Rogers' estranged wife.

They came over to her and introduced themselves as Lt. Bennett and Officer Cavanaugh of the Western Watch House in Baltimore.

"Do you know where we can find your husband?" Bennett asked.

Sally looked around the crowded lobby. "Could you ask the manager if there is a private room where we might talk? I have some interesting things to tell you. In fact, having read the article about the problems at Barnum's Hotel, my first stop when I arrived in Baltimore was to find you."

Surprised, Bennett asked and was given the manager's office for a short time.

The attractive woman of about thirty was quite candid.

"I am not his wife. I met him coming here on the stagecoach. My business is to entertain gentlemen. We had supper in the dining room, then he asked me to spend the night with him, which I did, in my room. On the stagecoach he held on to this leather case. I was very curious as to what it contained. During the night, I went to his room, picked the lock and found what I intended to bring to you today. It clearly identified him as the suspect you were looking for."

Sally reached into her purse and carefully removed the bulging napkin. As she handed it to Bennett, the pearls spilled into his hands.

"Do you suppose Lady Stafford might be offering a reward for the return of her jewelry?"

Both men were astounded, and at a loss for words.

"Do you know where he is?" Bennett finally asked.

"I haven't seen him since I went to get a refund on my locomotive ticket. I've been sitting here for a while, but he hasn't come in."

"He does know that you had the jewelry?"

"Oh yes. I have been careful not to be alone. I'm so relieved you have the pearls now."

"It just so happens Lady Stafford is up the street with her lady's maid shopping. You and I can return the pearls to her and you may ask her about a reward. Officer Cavanaugh, you find the local police and get a search going for...we know him as Robert Jamison. I want to confiscate his baggage and case. Ask the manager if we can secure it here in his office for a while. We will try to apprehend him when he boards the stagecoach."

Bennett couldn't believe his good fortune. "There is some paperwork we have to do, Mrs. Timmons. I will give you a receipt for the jewelry, which we will return now. Then you will come with us in our carriage back to Baltimore after we have Jamison. I need you to sign a statement at the Watch House. We also request that you stay in Baltimore for a short time, if possible."

"I would be under police protection?"

"Absolutely. Thank you very much for your honesty. Would you care to walk up the hill a short distance? I would like to catch Lady Stafford while she is here in town." He didn't relish returning the distance to the Manor.

Sally agreed, and they left Cavanaugh to make sure the Ellicott's Mills police would watch the terminus, the private carriages for hire, and the Railroad Hotel for Jamison.

Lady Stafford couldn't stop Becky from jumping from the carriage to go to Rocky. The cat permitted Becky to pet him as he purred contentedly. At last Joshua came outside.

"Becky! What are you doing here?" He was astonished to see her.

"I'm in town with Lady Stafford for some shopping. We saw Rocky and had to stop. I'm so happy to see you, Joshua. Come meet the Baroness."

Lady Stafford sat in the carriage as Becky introduced her love through the window. What a nice young man, the Baroness thought, but it brought tears to her eyes to see him loaded like a pack animal.

"Both of you please come into the carriage, and bring the cat."

Joshua took off his pack and left it with the coachman. They sat together chatting for some time, then the conversation turned to what Joshua really wanted to do in life. Lady Stafford mentioned that her father, Mr. Caton, might be able to put in a good word for him with someone at the Baltimore and Ohio Railroad. Joshua seemed embarrassed.

"Oh, I wouldn't want you to put yourself out for me, ma'am."

Lady Stafford was enjoying the eye language of love between the two young people.

"Why not let someone help you if that is really what you want? It would be a small matter for my father."

"Could I then do something for you in return, Lady Stafford?"

"That isn't necessary, Joshua," she replied, quite surprised. "It isn't a certainty that the position will be available to you."

"I understand." He reached into one of his pockets and brought forth the packet that contained the lovely lace trim that his mother had made, and given him to sell on the road. He handed it to Lady Stafford who was deeply touched.

"My mother made it."

"Thank you so much, Joshua. I will treasure it."

There was a knock at the carriage door, and Lt. Bennett, with a woman, said he had something important to tell the Baroness.

"Becky, you and Joshua and Rocky take a little walk. Say your goodbyes for now, and exchange addresses. Use the Greenspring Valley one for the time being. Goodbye, Joshua. We will be in touch. Take care."

Joshua and Becky gave up their seats to the lieutenant and Mrs. Timmons after a brief greeting. Bennett, with a great amount of satisfaction, handed the elated Lady Stafford her expensive black pearls.

Chapter 13   The Storm

Lady Stafford and Sally Timmons scrutinized each other as Lt. Bennett repeated the story of the finding of the pearls. Mrs. Timmons had never seen a Baroness before, even if she was an American, and Lady Stafford had never met a self-proclaimed prostitute. There was a more gentle term, "kept woman" for some of her European acquaintances who were being supported by men who were not their husbands. Even her sister, Mary Ann, had once had a scandalous relationship with the Duke of Wellington who tired of her, then recommended her to his brother who married her. Lady Stafford had to admit to having her "admirers" or she wouldn't be sitting here at this moment holding her pearls.

"Mrs. Timmons asked me if you might be considering a reward for the return of the pearls," Bennett asked the Baroness.

"I'm certainly very grateful, Mrs. Timmons, and appreciate your honesty. I think you do deserve a reward, but I will have to discuss the amount with my husband, the Baron. Perhaps we can work through Lt. Bennett on the matter."

"I would be very appreciative, Lady Stafford. Having the pearls in my possession was becoming very dangerous."

"If you would please sign the receipt for the pearls, Lady Stafford," said the lieutenant, "we will leave you to your shopping. We must return to the Railroad Hotel and try to find Jamison."

"Thank you both so very much," the Baroness smiled. "I have to find those two young people walking a cat. I believe it might be going to rain."

Becky and Joshua held hands as they walked partly down one side of the street and then back up the other side. Rocky strolled behind except when Joshua picked him up to cross the crowded road.

"Are you going to do the peddling again next week, Joshua?" Becky asked.

"I don't know. If I can empty this pack before I get home, it might be worthwhile. So far, I've been lucky with the weather, and the places I've stayed. It will seem lonely, though, without you."

Becky squeezed his hand. "It may take weeks before Mr. Caton can give you any news."

"And I have to be prepared for disappointment."

"I would love to meet your family, Joshua."

"So, you can, when you finally return to Baltimore before sailing to England."

"Don't talk about that. Maybe I could stay on here and work for Mrs. MacTavish."

"You would leave Lady Stafford?"

"If you asked me to, I would, although she has been very good to me. She would want me to be happy. I love you, Joshua."

"I know, and I love you, Becky. We're just very young to be making such lifelong decisions, and of course, I have no money."

"But you have to be positive!" Becky insisted. "I know you will get the job you want on the locomotive."

"How much longer will you be in Maryland?"

"About eight more days. Tomorrow we return to Castle Thunder, then to the Caton home in Greenspring Valley, then England."

"Letters will have to suffice, but we will see each other again, I promise," Joshua said with a lump in this throat.

A few drops of rain began to fall. The sky was turning dark.

"Joshua, you and Rocky are going to get wet. I hope you find good shelter tonight."

"Don't worry about us. We won't melt," he laughed. "Let me walk you back to the carriage."

Lady Stafford was waiting anxiously for them so she and Becky could return to the Manor before the storm broke.

After a tender public kiss, Joshua helped Becky into the carriage and said goodbye again to the Baroness.

Lt. Bennett and Mrs. Timmons joined Officer Cavanaugh at the Railroad Hotel.

"All means of travel are being watched by the local police," Cavanaugh reported, "in case he doesn't take the stagecoach."

"Let's check his baggage and case in the manager's office before it's time to load it," Bennett said.

Sally Timmons sat in the lobby with only about half an hour to go and watched for William to appear.

Nothing unusual was found in his baggage, mostly clothes, and his art supplies. Officer Cavanaugh asked Sally to come in and pick the lock of the case, which she did.

"I told you what was inside besides the pearls; his safecracking tools."

The manager called to them that the stagecoach had arrived and was unloading its passengers and baggage. No sign of Jamison. Other passengers boarded, but Sally returned her ticket for someone else to buy. Lt. Bennett asked the driver to wait five more minutes. Still no Jamison. The lieutenant told the driver to go on after another passenger bought the seat Jamison should have used.

"He will have to walk to Baltimore," Bennett commented. "Too shallow here and rough for any river traffic."

Sally's baggage was loaded on the carriage with Jamison's. She boarded with the two policemen. Sally was glad the pearls were gone, and a reward might be in the offering. The two men were happy to return to their regular jobs at the Watch House, although they might have to return to Ellicott's Mills for Jamison if he was caught there. Mark Bennett wanted to get home to Katherine and Jeremy, and sleep in his own house. A storm was brewing here, and he hoped they could outride it.

Joshua was the only one unprotected against the weather. For a short time, he and Rocky trudged along, heading for Catonsville. He tried to peddle at a few houses in a light rain, but it grew heavier as he left the Patapsco Valley, and walked uphill. The road was becoming mired from the rain, and Rocky meowed unhappily so Joshua placed him inside his jacket. In the distance, near Thistle Road, was a farm where the peddler had stopped on the way to Ellicott's Mills. No point in going any farther as the rain was becoming a downpour. A large barn looked perfect for spending the night. He would have to make a deal in peddling stock for a meal and a warm, dry bed in the hay.

The same woman he had sold to before opened the door to him on her porch.

"On the return trip, you got caught in the rain," she grinned.

"Could we make a deal for a meal and a night in your barn?"

"I did see some fancy shoe buckles I took a liking to, a few days ago. Do you still have them?"

"I think so," said Joshua, opening his coat and reaching into a pocket. Rocky's face appeared, and some of the woman's children crowded around to see the cat.

He handed the packet of buckles to the woman and she selected a pair.

"I have some rabbit stew and bread. One of my boys will bring it out to you in the barn. I'll also send out a clean blanket so you can take off your clothes and dry them off. Would you like a bucket of water and a towel to wash?"

"Yes, please, ma'am. Do you need any help tonight or in the morning?"

"My husband has tended to all the animals for the night. You might give him a hand in the morning if he requires some help, depending on the weather. Barn door is unlocked. Here, take a lantern with you."

Joshua thanked the woman, went inside the barn and let Rocky down on the floor. While he waited for the boy to bring the things from the house, the peddler made a comfortable pad with the hay, and took off his pack. This would be his last night on the road. He should make it home in time for shabbes tomorrow night. He wondered if Becky had returned to the Manor without any mishap in the rain. Joshua would write to her on Saturday, or drop a note by Castle Thunder in the morning.

The young boy, about fourteen, came in quietly and gave Joshua everything his mother had promised, making two trips. He hung about, and petted the cat, not in any hurry to return to the house.

Joshua decided to strike up a conversation with the boy.

"What is your name?"

"Ethan."

"Mine is Joshua. You in school?"

"Out now for the summer to work in the fields. Do you like being a peddler?"

"This is my first trip. It's not what I really want to do."

"I want to work in a mill," Ethan said. "I don't like farm work. What do you want to do?"

"Drive a locomotive," Joshua said with a deep sigh.

"Why don't you do it, then?"

"Too many people want the job. Doesn't your father need you here?"

Ethan shrugged his shoulders. "I have other brothers who like farming. If you have time in the morning, and the weather improves, I will show you a grand view of the river and the train tracks from high up on our farm."

"I would like that very much, Ethan. Thank you for bringing me my provisions. I think Rocky and I will eat our supper and settle down for the night."

Katherine had a message by the afternoon stagecoach that her husband, Mark, and Officer Cavanaugh would be home in the evening, but not to count on supper as he would have to go first to the Western Watch House to file a report. She had napped and was rested enough to think about going over to see Edith, Richard and the children. Jeremy went with her after their supper. He was anxious to meet Abby, so they hired a hack and got there after the Coughlin household had finished supper.

Richard seemed accepting of the idea of giving shelter for a while to the two orphans as he probed their situation with the law. This would take time, and Edith thought the longer they stayed, the harder it would be to let them go. She was happier than Katherine had ever seen her, and Abby and Pat were delighted to be reunited.

"I want to take them tomorrow to the second-hand clothing store," said Edith eagerly. "You know I can't sew very well, so that is the best solution. They don't have very much, and most of it is worn or outgrown."

"Did you enjoy your supper tonight?" Katherine asked the two children. With bright little faces, they nodded and smiled. Jeremy was close in age to Abby, and suddenly acted shy.

"Mark will be home later tonight. I really missed him being away. He has made some progress on the case. He will tell me about it later." Katherine sat back in the chair; her back was beginning to ache. Richard brought two cups of tea into the parlor for Katherine and her son. The herbal brew soothed her as she watched the new family, which she hoped would be permanent. Her thoughts turned to finding a woman to help her after the delivery and during the recuperation. Edith would have her hands full now, and time was getting short. On her next visit to the doctor, she must ask him to recommend someone.

Robert Jamison woke when he heard a terrible pounding of rain on the roof of the chapel. He opened his eyes to darkness and couldn't remember where he was. All he knew was that he was drenched in perspiration, extremely thirsty, and his hand was very painful. He had to relieve himself so he stood up in the darkness and tried to remember where the door was. The interior of the chapel was slowly returning to his memory and he knew there were some candles on the altar. He stumbled in that direction and felt over the cloth of the altar until he found them, but there was nothing with which to light them.

How could he have slept so long? He had missed his stagecoach and what had happened to his baggage and case? Sally would be long gone to Baltimore and the pearls with her. He would never find her again. This whole effort was wrecked, and he was running very low on money. As he felt his way along the walls, he finally came upon the door, but when he opened it, a gush of rainwater hit him in the face. He shut the door quickly, then unable to control the urge to urinate, let himself go in a corner of the room.

Were any lanterns lit outside? He thought he had seen some light coming from the bridge. The only window inside was the stained glass window. If he could wait until the morning light, he might get to the Railroad Hotel, and collect his baggage and case. If he could get himself another room, he could clean up, have something to eat and drink, and visit the doctor again. More stagecoaches would be running tomorrow, and maybe the locomotive tracks were clear of the rockslide.

He slumped down into the cushioned pew, trying to sleep, but the sound of the storm would wake the dead. His thirst was unbearable. He could hear the river crashing against the shore. He would make a dash for the edge, cup his hands and drink deeply. Flinging open the door, he left the chapel and found he could hardly walk for the mud and the blinding rain. He knelt down on the shore, cupped his hands, and drank deeply from the raging Patapsco. In an instant, he had spat out the muddy water, then lost his balance. He slid down the slippery bank into the rock-strewn water, trying to keep his head up.

Jamison tried to grab at some rocks, but they only tore at his hands, ripping away the bandage, and exposing the injury to more damage. He was a strong man, and he tried not to panic, but ride with the swift flow. Through the sheet of water, he could see ahead of him a small island in the middle of the river. He was cut badly all over his body by the rocks, but he managed to keep heading for ground. At last his body was blasted onto the green oasis where he clung to a tree. The river swirled all around him, but he felt he was safe for the time being. He was panting so hard he thought he would burst. Jamison turned on his stomach, still clinging to the bending tree, and hoping he could outlast the storm.

Chapter 14 Desperation

In the evening, back in Baltimore, Officer Cavanaugh registered Mrs. Sally Timmons at the McHenry Arms, a small hotel near the Western Watch House. He made sure Officer Blair would be on duty throughout the night. Supper was ordered from the dining room and sent up to her room.

"Rest tonight, Mrs.Timmons," Lt. Bennett said before he continued on to his office. "In the morning, you can sign a statement and have a formal interview at the Watch House." He was certain that she wouldn't cause any problems. She very much wanted a reward for returning the pearls to Lady Stafford.

It had been a rough journey from Ellicott's Mills to Baltimore. The rain had caught up with them early on and slowed the thirteen mile journey. Immediately on his arrival, Bennett had sent a message to Katherine by Officer Pierce that he would be home later in the evening. Captain Campbell had returned home so that was a blessing. The lieutenant could do his paperwork in peace.

Bennett had some supper sent in from a local eatery, and sent Cavanaugh home for the night. For the next two hours he worked on his report covering the last two days in Catonsville and Ellicott's Mills. He could hardly keep his eyes open and caught himself nodding off over the scattered papers on his desk. The captain would find this report on his desk first thing in the morning, then Lt. Bennett would appear with Mrs. Timmons for questions, discussion, and statements with Captain Campbell. Unfortunately he had not apprehended Jamison, but at least, the pearls had been recovered and returned to the rightful owner.

Leaving his office at ten-thirty, Bennett returned to his house on Liberty Street. Everyone was asleep and he checked the two bedrooms to find Jeremy alone in his bed, and Katherine in a deep sleep in their bed. He took off his clothes, washed, and climbed into bed, reaching out to his wife, contentedly, and hoping being away from his family would not often occur. Katherine stirred and sighed as Mark held her in his arms and kissed her hair. He wondered about Pat, and the sister, but both fell into a very deep sleep, so questions would wait until morning.

Joshua could barely sleep for the storm overhead. Even Rocky was restless and finally climbed into the peddler's arms for protection. The barn leaked and Joshua thought of his nights at the Piedmont Hotel in Catonsville, and the Cliffside Inn near the Manor west of Ellicott's Mills. Thoughts of Becky were also keeping him awake. The kiss outside the carriage was not socially acceptable. He supposed they had shocked the Baroness. He was surprised himself, but thoroughly enjoyed it, and knew Becky had been delighted. He wondered if he would make it home by tomorrow night when he was expected. Joshua thought about whether the rain would end in the morning, and all of them could get to their destinations safely.

Returning to the Manor, Lady Stafford had related to everyone there the unusual return of her black pearls, and an update on the case as provided by Lt. Bennett.

"But why did you go off and not tell us where you were going?" asked her sister Louisa, petulantly. "We might have wanted to go shopping with you."

"It was very thoughtless of you, Elizabeth," pouted Mary Ann. "I would like to have visited the bookseller."

"I must confess, my dear sisters, that Becky and I had no intention of shopping. She has met a young man who happened to be at first the Piedmont Hotel, and then the Cliffside Inn. They are very attracted to one another and Becky wanted me to meet him. It was rather like asking me for some motherly advice."

"So, did you approve of him, dear?" asked Mrs. Caton.

"Very much, but he needs help in securing the type of employment he seeks."

"That being what?" Mr. Caton asked.

"This is where you might help, Father. He wants to drive a locomotive on the Baltimore and Ohio Railroad, but there are too many applicants. I told him you might know someone in the company from a few years ago, who might put in a good word for Joshua on my recommendation." Lady Stafford looked at her father the way daughters do when they want something special.

"Well, I suppose I could send a letter in the young man's behalf to a particular board member. There are several I recall."

"Oh, thank you, Father. I have Joshua's address in Baltimore. He would appreciate it so very much."

"Elizabeth, dear," asked her husband, the Baron. "What is Joshua doing now to earn a living?"

The Baroness hesitated. "He travels about selling a general line of merchandise."

"What sort of merchandise?"

"Becky has fallen in love with a peddler. I do believe he loves her, and although they are very young, marriage might be on her mind." And I might be losing my maid, she thought.

"A peddler? Is he Jewish?" asked Mary Ann, taken aback.

"Yes, he is Jewish and works very hard at his job. I know you would all like him as much as I do. Now I need to talk about something else." She turned to her husband.

"Mrs. Timmons would like a reward for the return of the pearls." Lady Stafford had put them on in the carriage and was fingering them as she spoke with the Baron.

"Are you asking me to supply the reward for the return of a piece of jewelry given to you by another man?" he grumbled.

"No. I will be happy to take it out of my allowance. I really wanted you to suggest the appropriate amount to give Mrs. Timmons. Never mind. I will ask Lt. Bennett what he thinks." She should have broached the subject in private.

The family was embarrassed to hear this conversation between the newlyweds. Becky overheard the whole story from behind a door in the next room. She scurried upstairs to prepare her lady's clothes for packing for their departure back to Castle Thunder in the morning.

Later that night, lying in bed at the Cliffside Inn, unable to sleep with the storm, Becky replayed in her mind the events of the day. Hadn't he said he loved her, and kissed her unexpectedly in the street? That had been extremely bold of him. She hoped he and Rocky were safe, dry and warm. The rain had come on so quickly. Joshua did not have much time to find shelter. He must be somewhere between Ellicott's Mills and Catonsville. He would get by Castle Thunder first because he would leave earlier, and the Caton party would leave later and be farther behind. Of course, everything depended on the weather in the morning. Becky hugged her pillow tightly, wishing it was Joshua.

Jamison knew no one would find him until the storm was over. How could he survive? Only his head felt unscathed, except for a few cuts. The rest of his body was racked with pain from the pounding it took over the rocks. He felt some of his bones must be broken. The rain was washing the blood away from his gashes, but he knew he was losing a great deal of it. Jamison still had a terrible thirst, and he was cold, very cold. His arms were becoming numb from clinging to the tree. Could he last until morning? The man tried to wrap his legs about the tree, so he could rest his arms, and use them as a pillow for his head.

Never one to think about God, the thief and the murderer suddenly turned his attention to his Creator. Ranting and raving, he began cursing Him for letting him get into this situation. When he had gotten that out of his system, he tried to bargain with Him, promising to lead an honest life if God would rescue him quickly. Finally he remembered the stained glass window in the chapel depicting the Good Shepherd. Didn't he recall some story from his childhood about how the shepherd will leave the other sheep to rescue one who is lost? Here he was, lost and confused; fearing he was beyond all earthly help. Jamison began weeping uncontrollably, and sincerely prayed for the only time in his life.

Chapter 15   The Retrieval

A beautiful day was beginning in Baltimore. The heavy rain had washed the red brick houses and the cobblestone streets. Market wagons made their way to the various city markets while housewives wiped off their white marble steps, and compiled shopping lists.

Mark Bennett was up early, and so was Jeremy. Together they prepared breakfast for Katherine after having their own, and carried a tray upstairs to her room. Jeremy was then off to school, which soon would be over for the summer. Mark had a few moments to have a quiet time with his wife before facing Captain Campbell at the Western Watch House.

Katherine sat propped up in bed, enjoying her eggs and bacon and apple muffins. As she sipped her tea, she told Mark about finding Abby, reuniting the girl with Pat, her little brother, and how Edith and Richard had taken them in for the time being.

"I pray that they will be able to stay with your sister and Richard. If not, it would mean an orphanage or almshouse. Richard is not entirely won over, but Edith is, I think."

"Maybe over the weekend, we could visit them," Mark commented. "I would like to meet Abby. You know Richard is very level-headed and will check the adoption process, or being a foster parent before he commits himself."

"Oh, Mark, you have never seen Edith so happy before. I believe today they are going clothes shopping at the childrens' second-hand shops."

"Are you feeling well, darling?"

"I was tired yesterday, and my back has begun to ache."

"Promise me that with Pat and Abby somewhat settled, you will look into a hired woman to help you. I insist you ask Dr. Wright immediately."

"I will. Today I have an appointment. I missed you so, dearest. I hope you never have to be away again overnight. Tell me all about it."

Mark told her briefly about the last two days, the recovery of the pearls and the failure to find Robert Jamison.

Katherine wanted to hear about Mrs. Sally Timmons in great detail. "Did you find her attractive, Mark?"

"Katherine, she is a prostitute," he said indignantly.

"Do you have to have much more to do with her?"

"I have to take her to the Watch House today, and make sure she gets her reward in the next few days. She is only a witness in the case."

"Is she very thin? Does she have a beautiful figure?"

"Katherine, she is one tough lady in a refined sort of way. I like you nice and fat the way you are. You are extremely beautiful being pregnant. Now I have to go and pick up Mrs. Timmons at the McHenry Arms. Shall I tell her you are jealous?" teased Mark.

Katherine made a face, and threw a muffin at his retreating figure.

Sally Timmons was waiting for him in the lobby and was dressed fittingly for her excursion to the Watch House. Bennett couldn't wait for his captain's reaction to the lady of the night. They entered the Watch House and all eyes turned in her direction. The lieutenant deposited her in a chair in the main room while he went into Captain Campbell's office to discuss his report.

The robust sandy-haired, cigar-smoking captain was refraining from his nasty habit because he knew "the woman" in the case would be interviewed soon in his evil-smelling office.

"I am so very pleased that Lady Stafford has her pearls again," he began. "We will inform the manager at Barnum's Hotel immediately to alleviate any suspicion regarding their employees or guests, and put a notice in the newspapers to counteract any bad publicity. We can name the suspect finally even though he eludes capture."

Lt. Bennett sighed as his captain's pleasure went by the wayside.

"Please tell me in more detail why he hasn't been caught," the captain demanded, banging his fist on the desk.

"He simply disappeared on us, sir. We worked with the local police, had all means of transportation under surveillance. He should have boarded the stagecoach for Baltimore; his baggage and case were checked, his ticket purchased. The only way out was to cross the bridge and walk to Baltimore."

"I think that is what he must have done," the captain surmised with a frown. "The turnpike always has a heavy load of traffic between Baltimore and Frederick. Like our last killer in the ribbon case, he might be traveling in disguise."

Bennett gave the idea some thought, dismissed the disguise idea, and tried to remember exactly what was on the other side of the bridge. There was a sign: Oella. Someone had told him it was a small town in a rundown area, housing mill workers. Could Jamison be hiding there in a deserted house?

"Mrs. Timmons spent a fair amount of time with him. Perhaps we need to question her more about his behavior. She's a smart woman and she might have a theory."

"From your report, we have the statement ready for her to sign. Do you think, Bennett, we have any grounds to arrest her for prostitution?"

"Sir, you are forgetting that the act took place outside of our jurisdiction. She may deny it if she thinks she might be arrested. Ellicott's Mills isn't going to charge her with anything. It's so vague." The lieutenant wanted to leave that alone. "After all, she could have kept the pearls. She opted for a reward. She's been very cooperative."

"Very well, let's have her in."

Bennett ushered in the very attractive woman and introduced her to his captain. Officer Cavanaugh joined them with writing materials.

Very clearly the captain was confused. She didn't look like what he knew of prostitutes; from police business, of course. Mrs. Timmons was well dressed, refined and spoke like a lady. He decided to treat her as one.

"Please sit across from my desk." He held the chair for her. "We have a statement prepared for you to sign. Take your time to read it and ask any questions you might have before signing. I, myself, have two questions to ask you before you start."

The captain cleared his throat and ended up choking. Sally raised her head to Captain Campbell, waited for him to compose himself, then gave him a dazzling smile.

"Yes, sir. What would you like to know?"

"We are unclear about your marital status, Mrs. Timmons."

Sally sighed, and frowned slightly. "I am a widow, sir. For the past five years now. I have no children nor family. I am quite alone." She lowered her head and waited patiently for the next question.

Bennett didn't believe a word she said, but the captain was chagrined. "That's a pity to be without the support of a family." He gave her a benign smile, which turned out looking foolish.

"You had another question, Captain?" she asked demurely.

"We know you discussed the whereabouts of Robert Jamison, or William Rogers as you knew him, with Lt. Bennett, but you merely said you had lost track of him. Have you any theory as to his disappearance? You spent the most time with him."

"I have been thinking about that ever since we left Ellicott's Mills," she murmured. "Wherever he went, he had no other baggage than what was checked. The pain in his hand was becoming increasingly worse. I would think he would want to be close to a doctor for his daily treatment. I don't think he had any thought that he was under suspicion. I believe he might have walked across the bridge and met with an accident."

"You don't think he would begin walking to Baltimore?" asked Bennett. An accident had never occurred to him.

"His pain was beginning to sap his energy. He seemed uncomfortable standing outside in the sun while we were going between the terminus and the Railroad Hotel." She gave a short laugh and shrugged her shoulders. "Maybe he fainted and fell into the river. Walking was not in his plan."

Oella and the river. Those were two more possibilities to search, thought the lieutenant. He would get on to it as soon as possible.

"Captain, how long do you want me to stay in Baltimore?" Sally Timmons asked.

"What is your destination?"

"New York, I believe. Do you want me to stay until he is captured? And when do you think I may receive my reward from Lady Stafford?"

"I intend to send a message to the Baroness at Castle Thunder today, requesting her immediate intent as to the reward. I would like to catch up with her before she moves on to the Greenspring Valley," Bennett commented. "I'm sure Jamison will be found soon. Please give us a few more days. We may need you for identification."

"Don't worry about your expenses here, Mrs. Timmons," the captain added. "The police department will cover all your needs."

"Thank you," said Sally. "I will stay as long as you need me."

"There is just one favor, please," said the captain stiffly. "As you are under our protection and expense, we cannot have any other uh, um, persons visiting your room during this time."

"I quite understand, Captain Campbell," Sally said with a merry laugh. "I will be your model witness."

Before he left the farm near Thistle Road early Friday morning, Ethan insisted on taking Joshua over a field to see the view below them of the flour mills, the curve in the river,

117

and the train tracks crossing the river. Luckily, or perhaps Ethan knew the schedule, a freight train came along, blowing its whistle. It was a beautiful sight, encompassing the Patapsco Valley. The sun shone brightly after the awful storm of the night before, and everything looked sparkling clean. Joshua wished he was driving the train headed for Baltimore, but he still had a fair amount of peddling to do before he arrived home.

Ethan's mother bought a few more items and sent the peddler and his cat off after a good breakfast, not needing any manual help from him. He walked quickly and came to Castle Thunder an hour later. Having scribbled a quick note for Becky, he delivered it to the back door of the house. A servant told him he would give it to Mrs. MacTavish to give to Becky. Now Joshua really wanted to make time. He had seven miles to go before arriving at home, and he must peddle as much as possible.

The Caton family and servants arrived at Castle Thunder in time for a late lunch. Becky was delirious to have Joshua's love note and could think of nothing else for the rest of the day. Late in the afternoon, a message arrived for Lady Stafford from Lt. Bennett regarding the possible reward for Mrs. Timmons. While Mr. Caton retired to his room to compose a letter to a board member of the Baltimore and Ohio Railroad for Joshua, Lady Stafford began a message for Lt. Bennett. Deciding to settle this matter without the help of her husband, who had been rather cool to her since the episode regarding the pearls at the Manor, she enclosed her own personal check for $200.00, which was one tenth of the value of the pearls. She added that if Mrs. Timmons was not satisfied, to please let her know.

Elizabeth Caton Stafford, at first deeply hurt by her husband's display of anger regarding the pearls, had thought long and hard about his attitude during the carriage ride to Castle Thunder, and decided he was absolutely right. She had waited to marry until she was certain she had found the right man and that she truly loved him. It was wrong of her to wear jewelry given her by another man now that she was married. And there were other gifts of jewelry from men she would have to reconsider at home. The fate of the black pearls must be decided. Along with her message and check by stagecoach to Lt. Bennett, she sent another message to the Caton family jeweler in Baltimore, requesting an appointment in the next week.

A woman was the first to notice the limp body of a man wrapped around a bedraggled tree on a small island in a narrow span of the Patapsco River early Friday morning. Others crowded around the banks, mindful of the mud, and someone brought a long coil of rope. Two local policemen arrived, with high boots, and a battered door. Several men held on to one end of the rope as the two policemen spaced themselves along the rope, securing it tightly around their waists. The danger in getting to the island was not distance or depth, but the raging waters dashing over the slippery rocks. The end of the rope in front of the men was wrapped securely around the door. When the two men entered the water, with the door secured between them, the trick was to stand upright and walk carefully to the island between the rocks. To lose their balance would mean both men, trying to clutch the door, would be swept along downstream, probably cut to pieces on the rocks.

More men joined in on the muddy bank to secure the rope as the two men tested their footing. They only had to go about twelve feet to reach the island. The water came up to their thighs and the men cautiously, like tightrope walkers, edged their way around the rocks until they reached the island. They beached the door, then one man grabbed at a sturdy bush with thick wood to pull himself up on the bank. The first man helped the second one up, and both unwound the victim from the tree and turned him on his back. His eyes were open, but unseeing. The face was bruised and cut, but nothing compared to the body with much of the flesh in shreds, twisted bones, and the clothing badly ripped. One of the policemen felt for a pulse, but there was no life. Robert Jamison's soul had left the earth.

The body was lifted onto the battered door, and the men slowly retraced their steps through the river, pushing their burden forward. Dr. Miller, having been called to the scene, was waiting on the bank. He identified the man as William Rogers, one of his patients, and signed a death certificate. The police knew that this was the man Lt. Bennett from Baltimore was looking for, and their superior sent a message immediately to the Western Watch House regarding the death. The coroner appeared on the riverbank also and conferred with the doctor. Both agreed that the death was accidental as a result of the terrible storm, and there was no need for further investigation.

Unfortunately there was no identification on the body, no money clip or purse. Possibly the river had wrung identity from the man, and it might be lost among the rocks. If there were no family or friends to claim him, he would have to be put to rest in the charity cemetery on the outskirts of town. The local police would inquire of Lt. Bennett whether he had any other information about the victim, especially family to mourn him, and arrange for the burial.

Chapter 16 The Letter

"Mrs. Bennett, you say you are feeling well except for tiredness and a backache," said Dr. Wright, noting her good color, her active baby, and her not too excessive weight.

"Try to avoid the stairs whenever you can. Let your husband and son do errands for you."

"It is difficult when we live on three floors, and they often aren't home to help," answered Katherine, experiencing a slight bit of discomfort.

"Here is the name of a Mrs. Hopkins from your neighborhood. She is very good, and will come daily or live in for the time you need her. Of course, we can't tell her an exact date, but I would recommend you start with her a week before the delivery and set up a schedule. You are doing fine, my dear. Everything seems to be normal."

"Thank you, Dr. Wright. I will stop by her home when I leave."

Katherine went by hack, and found the woman returning from an errand. Mrs. Hopkins invited her in, and after an hour chat, the two women had all the details arranged. From there, Katherine went to the Coughlin home to see if Edith and the children had returned from their clothes shopping. It was close to three o'clock, and she was ready for a cup of tea.

Edith answered the door and was delighted to see her sister-in-law.

"Come in and see what we've been doing today!"

Abby and Pat were sorting through their bags, pulling out nearly new outfits. They smiled and kissed Katherine, then held up their clothes for her to admire.

"Put the clothes in the laundry room, children," Edith instructed. "Everything will have to be washed and ironed."

With the children in the basement, Katherine inquired how Richard and Edith were getting along with Abby and Pat.

"Oh, I love having them here, Katherine. Richard doesn't say much, but he hasn't objected to the extra expense, and he seems to like them enough. It will take time with him. You know how cautious he is. I'm simply planning on keeping them as if they were our own."

"How will you occupy them for the summer?" School would close next week until fall, and the city was already hot and humid.

"I will give them simple chores to do. They will have plenty of play time, and I want to start their schooling here at home. They are very far behind. You look pale, dear. How about some cake and tea?"

"Yes, thank you. I haven't eaten since breakfast." Katherine told her about her visit with Dr. Wright and Mrs. Hopkins, and Edith said she would still find time to help.

The children returned upstairs and stood by Edith like she was their mother.

"We're going right back down to the kitchen and bring up the tea things. I have a lovely chocolate cake."

Katherine rested and thought about this new family. She dozed off until she heard the clattering of dishes and voices ascending the stairs. The four of them sat happily down to afternoon tea. Katherine was so pleased everything seemed to be working out.

Having sent Sally Timmons back to the McHenry Arms with Officer Cavanaugh, Bennett reread her statement and sat at his desk to send off a few messages by the next stagecoach going west. Lady Stafford would have the one regarding the reward, and more importantly there was the note to the Ellicott's Mills police to try a search for Robert Jamison, alias William Rogers, in the Oella district, especially any vacant houses. He also suggested there might be a river accident. Little did he know that the police messages were crossing, one from Baltimore and one from Ellicott's Mills, on the turnpike.

After that, he decided to take a short walk to Lexington Market and get some late lunch. Friday was a busy day and he had to stand in line to get a corned beef sandwich, and again for a fruit drink, but he found a bench near the shambles outside, so he could have his lunch in the fresh air. How pleasant it was to eat outdoors, away from the hot, stuffy Watch House.

As he ate, he wondered how Sally Timmons would spend her time in Baltimore. She was free to come and go as she pleased. The only restriction was the one the captain had insisted on. Bennett would love to know the reason for her profession when she seemed so well bred. Her situation intrigued him, and did she fully understand how dangerous it was? His thoughts guiltily returned to Katherine. He hoped she had gone to Dr. Wright today. He decided to buy her some candy, and some for Jeremy. Reluctantly he returned to his office, trying to find a cool place to keep the candy until he returned home.

One could tell the weekend was beginning by the reports coming in to his desk. Most of today's crime was centered about the city markets where thieves had easy pickings among the crowds of shoppers, who were careless with their purses or loose cash in their pockets. One outside stall keeper at Lexington Market had a crate of live chickens stolen from him; no easy feat when chickens usually squawked their heads off. In an incident at a tavern, one man had been badly injured when hit with a whiskey bottle over the head. It was not unusual that the attack had been over a woman. A third crime was a deliberate ramming of one wagon into another, causing much damage, because of an argument about right of way in the street. The lieutenant assigned his officers to deal with these various lawbreaking events.

As he closed out his day, thinking of a quiet dinner with Katherine and Jeremy, Bennett was handed a message that had arrived from Ellicott's Mills. It was from the police and stated that the body of Robert Jamison had been recovered early this morning from the Patapsco River. Dr. Miller had identified his patient and signed a death certificate. There had been a terrible storm the night before and the man had met with an unfortunate accident. Did Lt. Bennett have any information as to notifying relatives? Bennett was relieved at this outcome. He had no sympathy for Jamison. Sally Timmons had guessed the truth. He went to tell his captain, who suggested that Bennett go back in the morning and tie up loose ends. Tonight a notice would go into the newspapers for tomorrow that the suspect in the Barnum's Hotel case had died in a storm in Ellicott's Mills. The case would be considered closed. Bennett wanted Sally Timmons to know, and stopped at the McHenry Arms on his way home.

Sally was coming down the stairs to have her supper at the hotel. She was pleasantly surprised to see Lt. Bennett coming toward her.

"Did you stop by to have supper with me, Lt. Bennett?"

"No. My wife is waiting for me at home," he replied, feeling a little foolish, and knowing he was being teased.

"Could we sit in the lobby for a few minutes? I have some news about Jamison."

He led her to a quiet corner where they would not be overheard. Sally sat, and the lieutenant sat opposite her with a serious expression on his face.

"He's dead, isn't he?" Sally asked, coming to the point.

"Yes, he is. I've had a message from the Ellicott's Mills police. He was pulled from the river this morning. You were the only one who suggested a river accident."

"I have had a feeling about it all day. I mean that he was dead. It was so unlike him to simply disappear on his own."

"The doctor, Dr. Miller, who treated him there, identified him. So few people really had any conversation with him; the Baron, perhaps Miss Cunningham, the two doctors, the hotel managers and you. You, most of all."

"Does that mean something special? Is there still a task to be done?"

"I'm not sure," the lieutenant answered uncertainly. "I feel something is unfinished. I have to return to Ellicott's Mills in the morning to answer some more questions. The police want to know of his family; who might come forward to claim the body, and pay expenses."

"Are you going by stagecoach or carriage?"

"No, I will take the morning locomotive, and return in the afternoon."

"Will Officer Cavanaugh go with you?"

"No, we need him at the Watch House. Weekends are heavy with crime." He had a feeling what her next question would be.

"May I go with you, Lt. Bennett?" she asked quietly. "I am your best witness, and I have nothing to do here."

Why not? thought Bennett. She was smart. Maybe she would notice something he had missed. Would he have to tell Katherine?

"You have been most cooperative, Mrs. Timmons. I accept your offer. I will check the locomotive schedule early in the morning, and send a message to you as to when we will depart. Do enjoy your supper and get a good night's sleep. It might be a long day tomorrow."

Becky Cunningham, with the other personal servants, arrived back at the Piedmont Hotel in Catonsville, enjoyed their supper, then the front porch rockers. Tomorrow was Saturday, and at Castle Thunder there would be much preparation for the next journey to the Caton home in Greenspring Valley. After Mass on Sunday, they would leave and she would be moving farther away from Joshua. She treasured his note, and hoped he and Rocky had arrived safely and in time for his family's religious observance.

What a dreary time it was here without Joshua. Would he forget her since he was back in his own surroundings? The note said otherwise, but long distance romances seldom survived. Lady Stafford had mentioned going into Baltimore one day soon, so maybe they might meet Joshua in town or visit at his home. At least she was fortunate to have her lady to help them. She knew what Joshua would say if he was here; she had to be patient.

Joshua arrived home one hour before shabbes. His pack was empty, although he still had a small amount of stock in his jacket. Sales had been good along the way, and his parents were pleased. They tried to shut the door in Rocky's face, thinking he was just another stray cat from the street looking for a meal. Joshua picked him up and declared him as his own. Mr. And Mrs. Asher were not very pleased, although Joshua's sisters adored having the cat.

The girls tried to keep their distance from their brother; a bit grungy, they thought, and he was growing a beard! No, he just hadn't bothered to shave while he was away. Mrs. Asher sent him up quickly to wash and change his clothes. Some other relatives joined them for the Friday evening service, and then they had a late supper.

Afterwards, the family listened to Joshua's week of peddling; the gypsies, Becky, the Baroness, the theft of her jewelry and its return. He ended with the promise of the Baroness to have her father, Mr. Caton, try to secure a job at the railroad for him. Mr. And Mrs. Asher smiled at one another, and his sisters began to giggle.

"What's so funny about that?" Joshua asked indignantly.

His mother took a letter from her pocket, and handed it to her son. It was from the Baltimore and Ohio Railroad.

"Your mother took the liberty of steaming it open," said his father, shaking his head. "She couldn't wait for your return."

Joshua tore the envelope open and read that if he was still interested in employment on the railroad, he should appear Monday morning at nine o'clock at the depot.

He had done it himself! Mr. Caton hadn't had time to get a letter to his contact, and this letter had been here for a few days. He would have to let Becky and the Baroness know, immediately. Joshua knew he wouldn't sleep tonight. His brief career as a peddler was over. He embraced everyone in his family, including Rocky. He had done it all by himself.

Before bed, when she gathered up the dirty clothes for the laundry, and sorted through the jacket to see what was left of the stock, Mrs. Asher noticed her lacework must have been sold.

"Did you get a good price for it?" his mother asked.

Joshua reddened, then confessed. "I didn't sell it, Mother. I gave it to the Baroness as a gift. She was trying to help me with the railroad job. She said she would treasure it."

Chapter 17   Return to Oella

Mark Bennett decided to wait until early Saturday morning to tell Katherine he had to take Mrs. Timmons with him to Ellicott's Mills. When he had arrived home in time for dinner Friday night, his wife was busy telling him about her visit to Dr. Wright and finding Mrs. Hopkins. Then she went on about visiting Edith and the children and how well things were going there. After dinner, he presented Katherine and Jeremy with the slightly melted chocolates from the market. They all enjoyed them, melted or not.

At last Katherine asked him about the case.

"As I was leaving, I received a message that our suspect, Robert Jamison, was pulled from the river this morning, a victim of the bad storm last night."

"Did he drown, Dad?"

"I suppose. I'll know tomorrow."

"Is the case closed?" asked Jeremy excitedly.

"Almost. I need to return in the morning to work out a few details with the local police."

"Like what?" Jeremy persisted.

"Try to locate some of his relatives. Prepare for his burial."

"Oh, Mark," Katherine said unhappily. "I thought we could have at least part of the day together."

"I promise you on Sunday, after church, the three of us will do something special."

"What?" asked Jeremy.

Hard put to give an answer at the moment, Mark said, "It will be a surprise."

He was tired, and the day would be long in Ellicott's Mills. He wanted Katherine in a good mood in bed, even if he could only caress her.

"Jeremy and I will clean up the kitchen, my dear. Take your time going up the stairs and prepare for bed. We will be up as soon as we've finished."

"Why didn't you tell me last night that Mrs. Timmons would be with you today?" Katherine was having trouble getting out of bed, but resisted Mark's efforts to assist her because she was angry with her husband.

"I was afraid this would be your reaction," he answered bluntly. "It is important that she is there. She knew Jamison better than anyone. She is one more person who can identify him." He almost added that she was a very clever woman, but he didn't think that would go over well with his wife.

"I suppose Officer Cavanaugh will be there?" she pouted.

"No, he has other things to do."

"Just you two? Traveling out and back in the locomotive, having lunch together in Ellicott's Mills?" Katherine's eyes were flashing.

"And viewing a dead body. Don't make it sound like a day in the park." Mark was tiring of the argument.

"I believe I will spend today in bed," his wife said haughtily. "Jeremy can help me, when I need something."

"Maybe that is a good idea, Katherine. I think you have been overdoing it. On my way home, I will stop at Lexington Market and bring home some supper. Anything special you want?"

Katherine gave it some thought. "I will have some roast chicken, rye rolls, sweet buns and more chocolates. And please ask Jeremy what he would like." She pulled the covers up to her neck. Another pound or two wouldn't make much difference.

Mark leaned over to kiss her goodbye, but she quickly put her head under the covers. "All right, Katherine. I will see you tonight." He left the room, more than slightly irritated.

"Have a good time!" she called after him in a muffled voice.

Mark's first stop was the Watch House where he informed his captain, after checking the locomotive schedule west, that he was leaving with Mrs. Timmons to hopefully conclude the case in Ellicott's Mills.

"She is willing to return with you?" asked his superior.

"Mrs. Timmons says she has nothing to do here while she awaits the reward from Lady Stafford. I find her quite intelligent. She may notice something we overlooked."

"As long as we are paying her expenses, she might as well do some work for us. Only make sure you are not delayed and return this afternoon." The captain gave him a sly smile.

"Yes, sir. My wife expects me home for supper," he answered with some embarrassment.

Lt. Bennett sent Officer Pierce to the McHenry Arms to inform Mrs. Timmons that she would be picked up at nine o'clock by Lt. Bennett. This would give her time to have some breakfast first, and for him to check some of the paperwork on his desk.

Like yesterday, Sally Timmons was dressed very properly for her return to the mill town. They went to the station and the lieutenant bought two tickets west, and the two tickets for the return in the middle of the afternoon. They boarded the locomotive for the trip that would take one hour and fifteen minutes. After some brief conversation, Sally took out her romance novel to while away the time. It was noisy on the locomotive and seats were too close together for private talks.

Bennett wished he had brought a newspaper. He spent part of his time gazing at Sally, comparing her to Katherine. His wife was pale with dark brown hair pulled back with tendrils falling about her face. Her eyes were dark blue. Sally was the opposite. She had an Irish look about her. Her hair, caught back in a bun beneath a becoming bonnet, was strawberry blonde, and her eyes were green. She was pretty and probably the same age as Katherine.

Occasionally she would glance up from her book and smile at him. She wondered what kind of effect she was having on him. She thought he was very attractive with his slightly premature gray hair and dark brown eyes. She tried to imagine what his wife was like and if they were happy.

A few times, when their eyes met, Bennett would act as though he was trying to get her attention. He would glance at the passing scene, and indicate something not to be missed; a curve in the river, people and vehicles traveling the turnpike, another locomotive passing by. He decided he would definitely buy a newspaper in the town and spend the time reading or dozing behind it on the return trip.

They reached Ellicott's Mills and found out where the Coroner and morgue were located from the local police. Neither the police nor Bennett had any more information to give one another. The Coroner gave the lieutenant a copy of the death certificate, then took Bennett and Mrs. Timmons down into the basement morgue to view the body.

The sheet covering the victim was lowered to the middle of his chest. Sally took a brief look, nodded, then turned away. Bennett stared at the battered, cut body; the face being spared the most.

"As you can see, we have signed the death as accidental in the storm," the Coroner explained. "The doctor and I do not think it was a drowning, but death from exposure and loss of blood. I can also give you a short letter to that effect."

"Thank you. That's most important," the lieutenant replied.

"Since it is summer, we will have to bury him soon. If there are no relatives, or friends, it will be a charity case."

"That seems to be the situation. We have no information on him, nor has there been found any money on his person, I understand," Bennett added. "I believe I will call on Dr. Miller next."

"Dr. Miller is visiting in Baltimore this weekend. Wait for a few moments, and I will write that letter for you."

Walking down the street toward the Railroad Hotel, and the terminus, Sally Timmons seemed a little unsteady, and Bennett took her by her arm.

"I'm sorry you had to see him like that," Bennett commented.

"But I wanted to be sure. I became very fearful of him."

"Would you like some lunch?"

131

"Perhaps something light, and some tea, thank you."

They went to an eatery near the terminus, and both quietly lunched on soup and crackers and hot herbal tea.

"Everything happened right here," Sally said, looking across the road to the hotel. "I would like to know how he ended up in the river."

"It seems we won't find the answer," said Bennett, satisfied to end it.

"Oh, I don't think we have to give up yet," Sally persisted, revived by the soup and tea. "We have some time before the locomotive takes us back to Baltimore. Shall we try to retrace his steps?"

Bennett looked at her in surprise. "Where do you want to begin?"

"Right here at the terminus. I think we are talking about a very small area. I first noticed him missing when he didn't come in behind me to cash in his locomotive ticket because of the cancellation due to a rockslide."

They went outside and the lieutenant followed Sally as she walked to the bridge and went halfway across. She stopped and studied what could be seen from that point. On the other side, to the right, the turnpike curved past the flour mill and houses on the right side, then beyond her sight, made a steep incline out of the valley.

"I don't believe in this heat, William would attempt that walk."

On the other side of the bridge straight ahead was a small town. Sally and Bennett crossed the rest of the bridge, stopping several times to view the fast moving river on the rocks. In the middle of the river, on both sides of the bridge, were small islands, one of which she knew William had reached. The small town of Oella was ahead and to the left, running along the river.

Although the town looked shabby, the bank along the river was inviting with shady trees and what appeared to be a small chapel or church farther down the river.

"William wasn't the type who would hide like a rat in a deserted house, or ask for help in Oella. Remember, he did not know then that he was under suspicion from the police,"

Sally remarked. "Although I would imagine he had no use for religion, with the pain in his hand and the heat, he might have sought some rest while waiting for the stagecoach. He was no longer welcome by the manager at the Railroad Hotel, so he could have stepped into the chapel where it might be cooler and quiet."

They walked to the building and Bennett opened the unlocked door, holding it open for Sally to enter first. Both were immediately assailed by the odor of urine, so they walked about the small one room place of worship until she found the source in a corner. Sally studied the altar and the modest stained glass window, then turned and looked out over the cushioned pews. In the very front was a folded jacket, undoubtedly used as a pillow. Sally recognized it and handed it to Bennett.

"This belonged to William. He probably fell asleep here and that is why he missed the stagecoach."

Lt. Bennett was already checking the pockets. "Any money would have been in the pants pockets and lost in the river." He pulled out the locomotive ticket and the stagecoach ticket and also a claim ticket for his baggage and case.

"You can't do much with this, can you?" Sally asked.

"Nothing at all, but tell the local police."

"I wonder how often anyone comes in here," Sally mused, folding up the coat.

"When he decided to leave, it must have been in the middle of the storm and he slipped into the river," Bennett surmised. "Why did he have to use the chapel as a privy?"

"I don't think he would do that deliberately. He might have been confused in the dark. He woke up, wasn't sure where he was. No candles were lit on the altar. Maybe he became panicky."

Bennett couldn't help smiling. "You have it all figured out, don't you, Mrs. Timmons? I believe the police department should consider hiring women on the force. You've been quite a help, and I thank you."

"Do you think you could call me Sally?"

"If we can sit here for a few minutes and talk about you personally, you can even call me Mark."

They sat down in a pew in the back and the lieutenant began.

"Aside from the case, I find myself very concerned about you. Does what happened to you with Jamison not cause you very much alarm?"

"Yes, of course. You know I was upset and still am, but I usually entertain gentlemen, not murderers."

"How can you be sure of their character on such a casual basis? There are the risks of disease or pregnancy. There are sadistic men who might beat you, or steal from you, or murder you. Prostitution has its occupational hazards. In the end, most of the women don't live very long."

"I didn't plan to make it a very long career. Only long enough to save some money and buy a house. Then I would turn respectable."

Sally lowered her head and fidgeted with her purse.

Bennett cautiously took her hand, and she looked at him with a smile.

"You are a very attractive woman in a very refined way. What was your background? What brought you to this?"

"My life, Mark, has been a Greek Tragedy. I was raised by wealthy parents in Philadelphia, whose sole interest in life as I grew up was tormenting each other. My father was a womanizer and alcoholic. My mother was also an alcoholic with a deranged mind. Other relatives were not particularly helpful, or on the scene. I was an only child. When I was away at school, I was happy. When home, I took my refuge in my room with my books, or sometimes with my friends who I was mostly embarrassed to bring home."

"I met a young man when school was over, and married him to get away from home. He had an unhappy situation with his parents, so I thought we shared something in common, and we could be sympathetic to one another. He had a very hateful attitude to his parents, which he soon transferred to me, blaming me for all the things that went wrong in his life. He beat me and caused me to lose a baby in a miscarriage. I almost died, and I have been told I can never have children. He disappeared, my father drank himself to death and my mother ended up in an asylum."

"All the money in the family was gone. I had no way to support myself. I couldn't sew or teach or be a nursemaid. In the early days of my marriage, I had enjoyed the intimate relations with my husband, so I thought I could succeed as a prostitute. So after five years supporting myself in the only way I knew how, here I am."

"Sally, I want you to stop now. I will try to find you some employment. You will have to learn a trade," Bennett said forcefully. "You like to read. You could teach children or even adults to read. Half the people in this city can't read, or even speak English. Some of the newly arrived immigrants could really use your services."

"Yes, that might be something I could do. I like writing, and I keep a journal. It is a good way to express your feelings. To me, it is amazing what comes out of my head onto paper. I have read so many romance novels, I do believe I could write one." She continued to let her hand remain in his.

"Then do it. I'll help you to get a room in a boarding house, meet some nice people, get started on a new career." He gently removed his hand, but continued to sit very close to her.

"Your wife is a fortunate woman. I would be respectable in a minute if I could find someone like you." She gazed at him with her lovely green eyes.

"Thank you, Sally. My wife is home, about ready to deliver our first child, and a little irritable today because she does not care for you and me to be on this excursion by ourselves. I love her very much and always will, and am eagerly awaiting the baby."

Sally laughed. "Truly, you are an excellent husband."

"Seriously, Sally. That doesn't mean that I can't be concerned about you, or that we can't even be friends. Will you please consider what I am saying to you?"

"You really think I might live longer, Mark, if I change my ways? I'll give it some serious thought over the weekend."

The lieutenant stood up, followed by Sally.

"I want to take the jacket and the contents back to the police before we leave. You can tell them how you found them in the chapel."

"I would also want to tell them," Sally added, "to locate the person who cares for the chapel to clean up the mess."

The lieutenant and Mrs. Timmons boarded the locomotive for Baltimore in the middle of the afternoon. Bennett remembered to buy a newspaper for the ride to take his mind off his companion. She completed her romance novel on the way to Baltimore.

"Before I return you to the McHenry Arms," the lieutenant said, "I want to stop by the Watch House to see if we have any response from Lady Stafford."

Sure enough, he was handed a note on their arrival, and after reading the contents, handed Mrs. Timmons the check for $200.00. Sally was delighted and said she would write to thank the Baroness.

"I suppose I could leave now if I wanted," she said, "but since I can't cash the check until Monday, I will spend tomorrow doing some soul searching. Will you be here on Monday morning?"

"Yes, ma'am, and I hope you will give me the right answer."

Sally Timmons took a carriage back to the McHenry Arms, and after Bennett had written a report for his captain and put it on his desk, he thought about picking up their supper at Lexington Market. He hoped to find Katherine in a better mood.

Chapter 18   Changes

After Sunday Mass in Catonsville, the Caton party was ready for the long ride by carriage to Brooklandwood in Greenspring Valley. This would be the last stop before the three "American Graces," along with the Baron and servants, would return to England. Emily MacTavish, the younger daughter of Mr. And Mrs. Caton, would remain with her family at Castle Thunder.

Becky had one week left of her American trip. What could she and Joshua decide in that time? His message had arrived late Saturday, and Lady Stafford and Becky were delighted to hear of his letter from the railroad, and the interview to take place on Monday. Mr. Caton had not sent off his letter in Joshua's behalf, pending Monday's outcome.

Also on Saturday, Lady Stafford had made a definite appointment with the Caton family jeweler in Baltimore for Tuesday after trying to make amends with her new husband.

"You were quite right, my darling, to be annoyed about the black pearls. I will never wear them again." She smiled tenderly at the middle-aged man who had won her heart.

"You know, Elizabeth, I will buy you anything you want," he said lovingly, taking her in his arms. "I would like to think you wouldn't enjoy wearing gifts from previous lovers."

"It was unkind and thoughtless of me." She thought about the exquisite diamond tiara and necklace he had given her as a wedding gift when she became his Baroness. Then there were her wedding rings. What more could any woman ask for?

"I sent a $200.00 check to Mrs. Timmons as a reward. On Tuesday, I want to take the pearls to our Baltimore jeweler and sell them."

"Why don't you give them to one of your sisters or your mother?" he asked, kissing her on the neck.

"No, I don't want to see them on any family members. Besides, I may have some use for the cash."

"Are you thinking of Becky and her peddler?"

"How did you ever guess?" she laughed. "The money would give them a nice start in life, if they decide to marry."

In the carriage, Becky tried to compose a letter to Joshua. Her lady had advised her what to say regarding Tuesday. Becky was to go with her and they would spend the night at Barnum's since the ride was so long. Would it be possible to visit with Joshua and his family Tuesday evening? Becky and the Baroness could stop by after supper. If this is convenient, Joshua should leave a message at the hotel Monday night or Tuesday morning, and also directions to the Asher house. Then they could hear about his job if it was certain, and do some celebrating.

While Becky was trying to write her letter along the bumpy road, Joshua and his family spent a good part of Sunday walking about the harbor, watching the pleasure boats float along in the breeze. Then they turned their attention to the large anchored vessels, searching for the names and home ports from outside their immediate world. Throughout the last two days, the family had heard about the whole peddling trip, and Mr. And Mrs. Asher thought the trip had been worthwhile. They heard as much about Becky as anything else, and his parents regarded each other with raised eyebrows. All this was so very sudden and the young girl was an outsider.

"Are we going to meet Becky?" they asked with a great deal of interest.

"We hope to plan something like that before she returns with the Baron and Baroness to England next week. I think I want her to stay. We haven't much time to make decisions."

After walking home from the harbor, many of the Lombard Street neighbors were out on their front steps enjoying the gossip and news. Joshua filled them in with his busy week. They enjoyed hearing about the gypsies, and the rescue of Rocky, and descriptions of the towns along the way. He didn't mention Becky. That was private within his family. As they had for so many years, Mr. Asher and his son ended their leisurely day walking to the depot and looking at the locomotives.

When Mark had mentioned to Katherine on Friday night that Saturday wasn't going to be a day in the park for him, it made Katherine remember hearing that there was to be a Sunday fair in one of the city parks. It was to celebrate the summer solstice, and there would be refreshments, games, and pony rides. How the children would love it!

After Mark had left on Saturday, Katherine had Jeremy take a message to Edith suggesting both families, she now considered Abby, Pat, Edith and Richard to be a family, should attend. She would surprise Mark instead of the other way around. Edith heartily agreed and sent a return message by Jeremy to say that they would all be at the Methodist church together for services, then go on to the fair. Katherine, if she tired, could sit under a nice shady tree and enjoy watching the children at the festivities.

When Mark arrived home last night, laden with their supper order, Katherine was on the first floor stitching away at baby clothes. Mark thought she looked well rested, as she hugged her husband as best she could. She had decided that she would not mention his trip to Ellicott's Mills with Mrs. Timmons. She knew it must have been necessary and she was sorry for her childish behavior. The woman was absolutely no threat to her. Mark was gratified that the matter was closed. Jeremy, Katherine and Mark enjoyed their supper, and Sunday's plans were revealed to Mark. Good, now he would have a chance to meet Abby, and have a restful day. How good it was to be home.

Katherine thought as she watched Abby and Pat at the fair that probably they had never been to one before. Jeremy guided Pat around while Abby made a friend with a girl her own age. At first, the two families strolled around, sampling some lunch from the vendors and spreading out cloths under the trees to have a picnic. Mark and Richard tried their hands at several games of horseshoes as the children enjoyed

139

shooting marbles, playing hide and seek, and various ball games. The men helped the children onto the ponies as Katherine and Edith had a chance to converse under the trees.

"Richard seems happy being with Abby and Pat," Katherine commented.

"He can't complain of them being a problem. Mary Tracy certainly taught them manners and good behavior," Edith replied. "Abby acts the little mother with her brother. Once, Pat lost his temper over something very minor and Abby took him aside and told him the two would have to work on his temper. He hung his head and said he would do whatever she thought might help."

"Does Abby talk about her time much with Mrs. Martin?"

"Only to say she was overworked. It wasn't that Mrs. Martin was unkind to her, but simply too many babies to have to handle plus other chores. I wonder how Mrs. Martin is managing now. Poor Abby is nine going on nineteen."

"Have you started their schooling yet?" Katherine asked.

"We are just beginning. Since neither of them has had any schooling, it will be easier as they are both on the same level."

"Richard may make some comments to Mark about the children that Mark will repeat to me later."

The two women watched Abby break away from the other girl and come and sit on the grass beside them.

"Pat and I have never had such a wonderful day. Thank you both for rescuing us."

Both women were startled and very pleased.

"Have you ever been to a picnic in the park, Abby?" asked Edith.

"No, ma'am. Will we ever come again?"

"I certainly hope so, my dear. The world is full of pleasant places to go, and things to do, even very close to home."

Abby turned her attention to Katherine, her eyes very serious.

"May I ask a favor, Miss Katherine?"

"Of course, Abby."

"When your baby is born, may I come to your house sometimes to help you care for it? I know all about babies."

Katherine laughed. "Indeed you do. You are an expert!"

"Then I can come?"

"Certainly, Abby dear. I would be most grateful."

Later that night when Jeremy was in bed, Katherine asked Mark if Richard had made any comments about Abby and Pat.

"He told me he is quite pleased with them. Since it appears Edith isn't going to conceive, although they had been hoping and trying for the past five years, he will consider adoption."

"I have never seen Edith so cheerful," Richard had told Mark, "and the children are so well behaved. Why shouldn't we give them a decent life? To come home each night to a lively house will keep me young."

"How do you feel about Abby and Pat, Mark. Do you think it will work?"

"At this point, what is the alternative? I believe Edith and Richard will make excellent parents. Money is not an issue. The children are happy in their new home. Isn't it unusual for a nine-year-old to express gratitude the way Abby did today? Could any of us send them now to an orphanage or almshouse, or palm them off on another person who might take advantage as Mrs. Martin did?"

Katherine shuddered. "I would take them here before any of those things happened."

"No, you wouldn't, darling," said her husband, "because you are not in a position to do that in your condition. You know that and you have to let this be. You and Edith have worked this out together in the best way possible and it will succeed. This will bring us all closer together, and Jeremy and our new baby girl will have cousins with whom they will grow up together."

"And why do you keep thinking that the baby is a girl?"

"I will be perfectly satisfied with whatever God sends us, but if it isn't a girl, we will have to try again next year."

Sally Timmons woke early to the chiming of all the church bells throughout the city. She stretched herself in bed and tried to go back to sleep, but the bells persisted, and suddenly she wanted to be a part of it. She couldn't remember the last time she had been to church, but she left the bed, bathed, dressed very properly, and decided to go to the Episcopal church a few blocks away.

Inside the ornate Gothic building with the magnificent stained glass windows, she found a pew in the middle and saw a similar window as was in the chapel in Ellicott's Mills. The Good Shepherd. William Rogers, as she knew him, lost as he was, had not been rescued. Was there a chance for her? The organ struck the interior of the church like a bolt from heaven. The congregation rose and she opened the hymnal. An Episcopalian as a child, the hymns and prayers came back to her, and sometimes Sally could barely mouth the words, or sing the notes, she was so choked up. She was not going to go down like William. Leaving the church, the minister outside the door welcomed her, and asked her to return. She nodded her head.

She walked to the Washington Monument and sat on a bench. Sally overheard an officer of the watch tell a visitor that last evening a young woman had jumped to her death from the top. Sally tried to look up at the top, but she was so close to the monument that it was difficult. Another lost person in the world. Probably a man was responsible for the young woman's action.

Mark came into her mind. "No one has taken a real interest in me, or been concerned for me since I can't remember when," she said out loud to two pigeons searching for crumbs. "I will listen to him. I will live in Baltimore where he can be my mentor, if necessary."

The reward money would help enormously. With her savings at home in Philadelphia in the bank, she would return there tomorrow after cashing the check, then pack the

142

small amount of belongings she had in the one room she rented in a middle-class boardinghouse. Returning to Baltimore, there should be enough money, five or six hundred dollars, to buy a modest rowhouse in a decent section of town, including furniture and the bare necessities. Mark Bennett lived on Liberty Street. Something might be found close by, or maybe it would be better near the Western Watch House on Greene Street. Sally had no intention of annoying him, but it would be comforting to have him close by.

How would she sustain herself? Rent out a few rooms, teach some of the illiterate immigrant adults to read? That appealed to her. And a novel. Sally already had some good ideas for writing one. The ones she loved were very popular. The women who could read had so little romance or drama in their lives that the books were devoured a soon as they were published. Some suspense might make them even more interesting. She would begin tonight by putting some ideas on paper.

But it was such a wonderful day to be out and looking around. With a newspaper folded up in her large purse, she decided to have some pastry and coffee at a little coffee shop on Centre Street while scanning the advertisements for houses for sale. If there was anything promising, she could view it and make an appointment to inspect it when she returned from Philadelphia in a few days.

Her conscience was nagging at her about the petty larcenies inflicted on the men throughout her five year career. Having some funds, she thought of restitution, but anything she had taken had been converted into cash and saved, and she couldn't remember who the men were, if indeed she ever knew their real names. Tithing was a thought. Add up her assets and give one tenth to the church. On second thought, better save that idea until she was set up in her house.

Tomorrow she would call on Mark Bennett at his office and tell him her plans. Sally felt better about herself than she had for many long years. Remembering what Mark had told her about his love for his wife, she realized she mustn't allow herself to fall in love with the lieutenant simply because he had shown her some concern and kindness, but she was afraid it was already too late.

Chapter 19   The Watch House

At Brooklandwood on Monday morning, Baron Stafford approached his Baroness as she was writing a note to Barnum's Hotel in Baltimore to reserve a room for herself and her maid for Tuesday night.

"You are sending off for the reservation, Elizabeth?"

"Yes, my darling. Would you like to come with us?" she asked jokingly, knowing his dislike for shopping.

"Would you mind very much if I did?"

"Not at all. I'll reserve two rooms. Did you want to take along Ridley?"

"No, I don't need a valet for overnight. Ever since we left England, we have been traveling in quite an entourage. I would enjoy getting away alone with you and Becky overnight."

Lady Stafford frowned. "I'm sorry I am so overloaded with family. My sisters can be very tiresome at times."

"This is supposed to be a honeymoon of sorts. I wanted to come and meet all your American relatives and friends, but I think when we have settled down at home for a few months, we should consider a cruise on the Aegean Sea in the fall."

"What a lovely idea! Just the two of us except Becky probably won't be with us, so it will be someone new, and of course, Ridley."

"We do have plans to see Joshua tomorrow?"

"Becky's letter is going off with this note. She explains that we would like to stop and visit after supper at the hotel. She has asked for directions and a suitable time. Becky wants him to leave a message tonight, or in the morning, at the hotel about the job interview and if the Asher family can receive us."

"Yes, that sounds good. I'm very fond of Becky in a fatherly way. If she decides not to return with us, I will feel better meeting her friend and his family and knowing she is safe."

Joshua was at the depot before nine to have an interview and hear what the Baltimore and Ohio Railroad had to offer him. As he was completely inexperienced for the railway job, he was not to be a locomotive driver immediately. He would have to work himself up. He could be a guard, a porter, a booking clerk, a signalman, or a fireman with a few week's training. As the fireman job was the only one on the locomotive, all the others being on the ground, Joshua asked if he might train for that.

"You realize that it can be hazardous, young man," the officer for employment explained. "Your job is to stand and shovel coal into the firebox, and keep the boiler full of water. Sparks fly, especially if it is a windy day. Several times the sparks have flown back on the passengers and ignited their clothes. Thank God, none were seriously burned."

"Sir, I would like to be a fireman, knowing that someday I could work my way up to a driver. I really want to be on the locomotive."

The man, Mr. Weston, liked Joshua and had good recommendations from some of his neighbors, and his last employer where he had been a dishwasher. A salary was discussed, and the hours were set.

"I didn't think I had much of a chance. It was some time ago that I applied and I hadn't heard anything. I know you have many applicants."

"Yes, we do, but the railroad is growing by leaps and bounds. A whole new expansion is taking place. We have to schedule more locomotives all the time. Stagecoach travel and moving freight by road will be a thing of the past. So if you want to start on Wednesday, that will suit us."

"Yes, sir. That would be fine. I was in Ellicott's Mills last week and visited the terminus."

"Did you go by locomotive?"

Joshua smiled. "No, I walked from Baltimore to the terminus and back. I filled in a week by doing some peddling."

"That takes a good amount of stamina. Exactly what you need to work on the railroad." Mr. Weston stood up, indicating the interview was at an end.

"Did you know Andrew Jackson is the first president to travel by rail and it was on the Baltimore and Ohio between Ellicott's Mills and Baltimore in 1833? That was the end of stage travel for him."

Joshua followed Mr. Weston to the door. "I was unaware of that. That is a good recommendation coming from President Jackson. Thank you for hiring me. You won't be disappointed."

Sally Timmons arrived at the Western Watch House at nine Monday morning and was ushered into Lt. Bennett's office. Officer Cavanaugh did the ushering and waited by the door, hoping to hear their conversation.

The lieutenant thought she looked very refreshed this morning. Her eyes were sparkling and she was bursting with news. He invited her to have a chair, and decided it was a good idea to let Cavanaugh stay to keep the meeting on a strictly official basis.

"I have decided to take all your advice, Lt. Bennett. I am leaving for Philadelphia after I cash my reward check, and I intend to vacate my lodgings there. I will return here in a few days, and buy a rowhouse with the reward money and my savings. Then I may rent out a room or two, probably teach reading to immigrant adults, and write. A novel." All this was said with her barely taking a breath. She laughed and waited for his response.

"I am so very happy to hear your plans. I'm sure you will be very successful at whatever you do. Always remember that I will be available if you need any advice."

"And I will be available if you need help moving into your house," chimed in Officer Cavanaugh with a big smile.

Both Sally Timmons and the lieutenant looked at him in surprise. Cavanaugh looked embarrassed. "I meant with you being a lady and all alone."

Sally showed a new interest in Officer Cavanaugh. "That's very kind of you. Thank you. I will have to buy the house first, although I did walk around and look at a few that were advertised in the newspaper yesterday."

"And I can show you the good areas around town. That's what comes from walking a beat," the officer of the watch added.

"Don't you have some pressing police business to do?" ask his superior with a frown.

"Yes, sir, but when you return, Mrs. Timmons, remember I'm here to help." Cavanaugh reluctantly left the lieutenant's office.

Bennett turned to Sally. "I may have to put him on overtime."

"Please don't do that," Sally said with a smile. "I believe, if you really don't mind, I will call on him."

She stood up and looked at Bennett sadly. "I won't keep you any longer." She put out her hand and rested it on his arm. "Thank you for turning my life around. I hope I will see you again soon."

Bennett covered her hand with his as he walked her to the door. He thanked her once more for her help with Robert Jamison. Sally stopped, then stepped back, and whispered to the lieutenant.

"Don't worry, Mark. I promise not to seduce Officer Cavanaugh."

There was a lingering scent of perfume in the Watch House following Sally Timmons' departure. Officer Cavanaugh was talking to the duty officer at his desk as Bennett returned to his office.

"Would you please come into my office, Cavanaugh?"

The large, burly, gruff officer of the watch, the right hand man of Lt. Bennett, was reduced to a plush toy bear.

"First of all, you do not interrupt my conversations with witnesses, or try to ingratiate yourself with them. Are you...?"

The captain came out of his office, puffing away on a cigar, and barged into Lt. Bennett's office.

"I smell perfume, and I remember smelling it before. Mrs. Timmons has been here. Why wasn't I told?" He was red in the face and in another nasty mood.

"Yes, Captain Campbell. She only came to see me briefly to tell me she intended to purchase a house in Baltimore and put down roots. She has her reward money from Baroness Stafford and she has decided on a career change."

"Can we be sure of that?" he persisted, squinting through the smoke.

"I think she is quite sincere."

The captain looked at Cavanaugh. "What are you two talking about?"

The lieutenant explained that Officer Cavanaugh was offering some physical aid to Mrs. Timmons when she was ready to settle in her new house.

"Not on police time. Why would she want a whole house for herself?"

"I believe she wants to rent some rooms out," offered Cavanaugh. "She also mentioned teaching reading, and writing a novel."

"Don't you get any ideas about renting a room from her. I will want the house watched for some time to determine whether she is running a house of prostitution. At any rate, I want to be told if she returns to the Watch House again. She is a very pretty woman and we don't see many pretty faces in here. I would also have liked to thank her for her help with the case." He glared at his two officers. "Get back to whatever you were doing! Stop standing around and wasting time!" He stomped out of Lt. Bennett's office and returned to his own, slamming the door.

"As I was about to ask, Officer Cavanaugh, before we were so rudely interrupted, are you romantically interested in Mrs. Timmons? That would surprise me because I've heard you mention a lady friend before."

Cavanaugh grinned. "I have had many lady friends, Lt. Bennett, and I have one at the moment, but no one I have ever wanted to become shackled with in marriage."

"So how do you feel about Mrs. Timmons?"

"I think I fell in love with her the first time we questioned her. I know she was a prostitute, but she isn't anymore, and I haven't exactly been a saint." He thought about it for a moment. "You know, sir, having a policeman for a husband would certainly keep her in line."

Very late in the afternoon, Joshua received the letter from Becky. She told him she wanted to come with the Baron and Baroness for a visit tomorrow evening at the Asher home after supper. They were on an overnight trip to Baltimore and staying at Barnum's Hotel. Becky asked if Joshua would leave a note by early Tuesday morning at the hotel to let them know if that was agreeable with him and his family.

Joshua immediately showed the letter to his mother who was rather distraught that he was going to be a fireman instead of a driver on the locomotive.

"You will have nothing but burns all over your hands and arms. Wait until your father hears about this. He won't permit it." She had been crying softly and lamenting the situation to his sisters, Esther and Sarah, all afternoon. Suddenly she was given a letter concerning the arrival of a Baron and Baroness at her house on Lombard Street, and the tears quickly dried up.

"We will finally meet Becky. But what do I do with the nobility? What would we ever talk about?" Judith Asher began pacing the room. "I know. They must come for supper. I am at my best preparing food. We will have a wonderfully congenial meal, with good Jewish fare where we can have wine and relax and enjoy the company and food."

She looked at Joshua. "You have met the Baroness. Is she an easy person?"

"Very down to earth, Mother," he assured her. "You will like her. I really don't know the Baron. Becky seems to be happy with them." He was ecstatic that he would be seeing Becky tomorrow. "They request that I leave a note at Barnum's as you see in the letter. I can do that in the morning and mention supper if you don't think it is too much trouble."

"It will be a thrill for me, and an honor for the whole family. Your sisters will help. You write Becky the note and mention six o'clock for supper, and give them directions. I can't wait to tell the neighbors!"

"Please, Mother, don't tell the whole neighborhood. We don't want the visit to be a public event."

"What shall I serve them? I suppose chicken is safe. Mostly everyone likes chicken. Chicken with mashed potatoes, a green vegetable, and some of my special rolls. For dessert we can have rugalech. Your father can choose a sweet wine."

Joshua and his sisters agreed with her choice. He hoped the guests would enjoy the Jewish cooking.

"I'll put on my very best lace tablecloth and napkins. You told me the Baroness liked my lacework. That will be something to talk about."

"What should we wear?" asked Esther.

"Our good clothes, of course. This is a special occasion," Judith answered.

"What do we call them?" Sarah wanted to know.

"Becky calls the Baroness "my lady" and I suppose the Baron would be "my lord," Joshua replied.

"Ma'am and Sir might do," ventured Esther.

"That's good, dear. Nice and simple," said her mother. "I can't wait until your father gets home to tell him. First we will have to tell him the bad news about Joshua's fireman job. Why do we so often have the good and the bad together?"

"Remember, everyone," Joshua insisted, "we have to keep the visit to ourselves."

But Judith Asher had to tell somebody. Her best friend, Rose Soloman, would never forgive her if she found out after the fact. To tell one person wouldn't hurt. Who would believe this could happen on Lombard Street?

Chapter 20 Lombard Street

When the Baron and Baroness, along with Becky Cunningham, arrived at Barnum's Hotel late Tuesday morning, they found a letter waiting for them from Joshua Asher. They were surprised at the supper invitation, but delighted to accept the kind hospitality of the Asher family. After checking into their rooms, Lady Stafford took a few moments to reply by letter and send it off with a messenger from the hotel.

"We will have luncheon in the dining room," decided the Baron, "then visit the jeweler."

Becky felt more like a relative than a servant to her lady. Indeed, the Baroness had always treated her very well. She prayed everything would go well tonight with Joshua and his family. Not too many days were left before the return to England. She wanted some decision to be made regarding her future with Joshua.

After lunching on Crab Imperial, Maryland beaten biscuits, fried potatoes, white wine, and a fruit tart, they took a carriage to Charles Street, and entered the shop to be greeted by Mr. Ames, longtime jeweler to the Caton family.

"Why don't you and Becky look about the shop while I talk with Mr. Ames in his office?" Lady Stafford suggested to her husband.

"Very well," the Baron replied, following Becky around as she gazed attentively at the inside of the cases.

Inside the jeweler's office, in strict privacy, the Baroness brought forth the black pearls, told him she wished to sell them, and what might he offer her if he was interested?

Mr. Ames examined them very carefully, taking the pearls to a window for the light.

"Have you any idea what the original price was?"

"No. The pearls were a gift. I had to mention a value to the police because they were temporarily stolen, then returned to me. I told the police I thought perhaps two thousand dollars. That is what I insured the pearls for in England, of course, the equivalent for pounds."

"Yes, I remember reading about the theft and murder at Barnum's Hotel. It must have been most distressing for you." He paused as she nodded her head.

"The police handled the incident very well, and I have my property back."

"I think, ma'am, you have undervalued the black pearls, but you know, I must offer you a lesser amount for resale."

"Certainly. How much did I undervalue them?"

The jeweler continued to slip them through his fingers in the sunlight, noting the unusual color.

"I believe I would sell them for five thousand dollars, which means I might offer you twenty-five hundred."

"Oh, really?" murmured the Baroness, pleasantly surprised. "The fact that I was the previous owner would be unknown to the buyer?"

"Yes, of course. We protect our clients. Then you would accept my offer?"

"Yes, I believe I will. My husband does not particularly care for the pearls."

"I understand, Lady Stafford. May I also congratulate you on your recent marriage?"

"Thank you, Mr. Ames."

He gave her a check, and they left the office for the salesroom where she found her husband purchasing a small pair of aquamarine and gold earrings for Becky. Her maid was politely trying to discourage the gift, stunned by his generosity, but the Baron insisted the earrings were "only a trinket."

Lady Stafford smiled at them. "Wear them tonight, Becky. How well they match your eyes."

Becky was almost speechless, but managed a whispered "thank you."

In the carriage, Lady Stafford said, "Good riddance to the black pearls. Two men are dead because of their greed for them. I hope the new owner will have better luck."

After returning to the hotel, and a refreshing nap, it was time to bathe and dress for the evening. As Becky was styling her lady's hair and dropping hairpins on the floor, she began apologizing for her clumsiness.

"I'm so sorry, my lady, but I am very nervous about tonight."

"I have a feeling everything will turn out better than you expect. Before we leave, drink a small glass of brandy."

When the carriage arrived at the address on Lombard Street, the guests noticed a good number of people sitting outside on their front steps enjoying the cool summer breeze. Must be very warm inside the houses, thought the Baron. All conversation ceased among the neighbors and all eyes turned to the occupants of the carriage as they alighted in front of the Asher house. Suddenly a cheer went up from the people, surprising the guests. As the Staffords and Becky waited after knocking at the door, they turned, smiling, and waved. The Baron, noticing a small banner inscribed with a bright "Rule Britannia" whispered to his wife, "Have they forgotten about the War of 1812?"

Joshua answered the door, dressed in a fine black suit, and cleaner than Becky had ever seen him. How handsome he looked with his dark eyes and darker hair. Joshua took one look at Becky and almost melted with love. Her eyes looked unusually blue tonight. Becky introduced Joshua to the Baron whom he had never met, and the young man bowed to the Baroness. The guests were invited into the parlor where Mr. And Mrs. Asher and Sarah and Esther stood in what amounted to a receiving line. Jacob Asher bowed, and the women curtsied as the Staffords and Becky were introduced. How very attractive the Baron and Baroness were, thought Judith Asher. Becky was quite a beauty. No wonder Joshua had fallen for her. Judith Asher returned her attention to the nobility.

The Baron was of medium height with dark blond hair and lively blue eyes. The Baroness was small with a heart-shaped face, and curly brown hair, almost the same color as her eyes. She wore almost bohemian attire; a light, low-cut paisley dress with a matching beret. A silver necklace and earrings completed her costume.

They were seated in the parlor after the Baron had handed Jacob Asher two large bottles of cold champagne.

"I understand we have something to celebrate tonight," said the Baron. "Your son's new job on the railroad."

Judith Asher looked unhappy, but her husband concurred with the Baron and Joshua that indeed it was something to celebrate.

Most of the conversation before dinner centered on Joshua's experiences on the road, and the circumstances of the murder and theft of the black pearls, leaving a trail from Baltimore to Ellicott's Mills and beyond. Mrs. Asher served some appetizers with the champagne in the parlor, and all were quite congenial.

Rocky sauntered into the room, heading straight for Becky who picked him up, embracing him and kissing him on his head.

"How I have missed you, Rocky," Becky murmured. "Do you like your new home?"

Rocky purred away and looked over the Staffords carefully as he rubbed his face against Becky.

"Excuse me, please," begged Judith Asher. "My supper is ready to be served. Come along, girls." Esther and Sarah went with their mother while Becky and Joshua had a few moments alone with Rocky between them. The Baron and the Baroness discussed the clothing business in Baltimore with Jacob Asher.

Once they were all seated at the dining table, Lady Stafford commented on the lovely lace tablecloth and napkins.

"Joshua gave me a sample of your lacework. I will put it to good use in my new home."

Judith Asher beamed as she served them the supper she and the girls had been preparing since last night. More wine was served and compliments and conversation filled the warm room.

Afterwards, back in the parlor, the subject of the departure for England came up. In answer to a question from Jacob Asher, the Baron replied, "Saturday we sail. We've been away for several weeks, and my bride must take up her duties at her new home."

Becky gave Joshua a distressed look, and he rose to the occasion. He moved closer to Becky and took her hand.

"This is an evening which will probably never be repeated due to the ocean between us." Also he thought to himself, the social barriers that we have broken tonight. "Before all assembled here, I would like to ask you, Becky, to be my wife." Quickly he added, as he glanced at the lady's maid, "As you know, all I have to offer you is the fact that I have a new job."

Becky flung her arms around Joshua's neck, and gave him a kiss, causing a few raised eyebrows. "I accept, Joshua, with all my heart."

Everyone, some hesitantly, clapped, and Becky was embraced by each member of her prospective family, and the Staffords. Jacob Asher, in the excitement, forgot formality and slapped the Baron on the back, but stopped short of touching the Baroness.

"We need time to introduce Becky to the neighborhood and teach her our ways. This can't be rushed," said Judith Asher.

Lady Stafford exchanged a smile with her husband.

"Yes, Becky will have to learn all about her husband's heritage, religion and customs. She will have to be accepted, and Joshua will also have to be tolerant." The Baroness turned to Joshua's mother. "After tonight's wonderful supper, I'm sure you will teach her to cook, and Esther and Sarah will guide her along the way." She looked warmly at Becky sitting on the sofa, holding hands with Joshua.

"We regret that we will be unable to attend the wedding, but before we leave, the Baron and I would like to give Becky and Joshua a gift to help them in their new life. We intend to deposit into an account for you a $1500.00 check which will buy you your own home, and furnishings."

There was dead silence in the room as the Asher family and Becky took in the news. Becky rose and went to the Staffords, giving each a hug. Joshua, slightly dazed, followed Becky and expressed his thanks. The Ashers were at a loss for words.

"Now the next thing to decide," Lady Stafford continued, "is where you are going to stay, Becky, after we leave on Saturday."

The Asher family waited for the Baroness to decide, feeling events were moving too quickly.

"Becky could stay with my sister, Mrs. Emily MacTavish, in Catonsville. It is only seven miles away. Joshua and Becky could arrange to meet when he isn't working and she is also free. That would be proper. Wedding plans could be shared among the two houses. There also needs to be time for house hunting. If you feel I'm making too many decisions, it's because Becky's mother isn't present, so I am trying to stand in her place."

Joshua and Becky glanced at each other. Seven miles was a great distance to them.

"This has been enough excitement for one evening, and I believe it is time for us to say goodnight," said Lady Stafford. Everyone needed some time to absorb the engagement.

As the Staffords and Becky left the house, they saw a few lingering neighbors still on their steps. The waving continued until the carriage was out of sight. Inside, as they rumbled across the cobblestone streets, Becky spoke about the Stafford's generous gift, and how much she would miss them.

"When I return to England, I will contact your mother and explain to her what happened. I'm sure, though, you will write her immediately."

"Yes, my lady, tomorrow."

"I will arrange for your mother to attend the wedding."

"That would make my day complete. You think of everything, my lady, and I will enjoy helping Mrs. MacTavish in any capacity."

The Baroness sighed. "Becky, you have chosen a very nice young man with a loving family. I know you will be happy. My advice to you, and you have the means now, is to start off on your own. Be mistress of your own house, and not overwhelmed by family. Young people need their privacy. I shall hate to lose you, but maybe you will visit us one day, or we will be back again another time for a visit."

"May I say something, Elizabeth?" asked the Baron.

"Of course, my darling. What is it?"

"This evening, with the Asher family, has been the most enjoyable time I have spent on this trip. Their warmth and hospitality are so genuine."

"Yes, I quite agree. We leave Becky in good hands."

On Friday, Katherine Abbott was walking along Greene Street, about to enter Lexington Market. She noticed Officer Cavanaugh coming toward her with a very attractive woman on his arm.

"Why Mrs. Bennett, how are you?" smiled the policeman.

"Fine, thank you, and you?"

"Quite well. I would like you to meet my friend, Mrs. Timmons. Sally, this is Lt. Bennett's wife."

Katherine immediately went rigid. For some reason she had assumed Mrs. Timmons had left town. Mark and Katherine had not spoken of this woman since Katherine's outburst in their bedroom. Each woman appraised the other while exchanging pleasantries.

Finally Mrs. Timmons said, "Michael, Mrs. Bennett looks uncomfortable. Let us not keep her standing here any longer."

"Yes, of course. Beg pardon, Mrs. Bennett. We have some houses to view along this street."

When Mark returned home in the evening and supper was over, Katherine told him about her encounter with the policeman and the prostitute.

"I was surprised they were on a first name basis," his wife said. "Now that the case is closed, why is she still around?"

"Cavanaugh is besotted with her. Told me he fell in love with her the first time he met her."

"Are they going to marry? Is that why they are looking at houses?" Katherine was being very persistent.

"From what I've been told, Mrs. Timmons has moved from Philadelphia to Baltimore. She is looking to purchase a house, and give up prostitution in favor of teaching reading to immigrant adults. She also wants to write a romance novel." Mark hoped Katherine wouldn't ask how he knew this, wanting her to assume all the information came from Officer Cavanaugh.

"Oh, like a Jane Austen novel?"

"I don't know. She is quite a reader."

"Is he house hunting with her on police time?"

"No, he knows better than that. Today was a half day for him. He is supposed to be only assisting her in her search."

Thankfully, before Katherine could continue along this line, Jeremy came bursting in the front door.

"I was out collecting some of my newspaper money, Dad, and there is a small group of street boys hanging about the gaslamp at the corner. I'm sure they are pickpockets."

"Do you see an officer of the watch anywhere on the block?"

"Well, a block away."

"Go down the street and tell him what you told me. He will take care of it. Remember, you can't arrest them. Please do not bring any of them home!"

"Yes, sir. Back in a minute."

Katherine and Mark burst out laughing. "I believe Jeremy is going to follow in your footsteps," Katherine said.

"We are about to have fifteen minutes of quiet. Do you think we could sit by ourselves in the parlor and have some peace?"

He pulled her by the hand, and plumped some pillows behind her back on the sofa. She reached up to him, put her arms around his neck and drew him to her. As he started to embrace her, she took his hands and placed them so he could feel the baby moving about.

"I think our daughter is coming early. She has been unusually active today, and appears to have dropped."

Mark looked at her with concern as Katherine took a deep breath and closed her eyes.

"But you have a few weeks to go."

A sharp pain caused her to grab his arm. "Babies can arrive early or late. When Jeremy returns, please send him for Dr. Wright."

It was a long night at the Bennett house on Liberty Street. After the doctor arrived and examined Katherine, he sent Jeremy for Mrs. Hopkins. In the excitement of the impending birth, Mark forgot to wind the clocks as he did each evening. When baby Kate arrived at five minutes to five in the morning, the shelf clock on the parlor mantle stopped.

Chapter 21   Brooklandwood

Mr. and Mrs. Farrell watched the two departing carriages leave the grounds of the Caton estate. Mr. Farrell, tall and gaunt, was in charge of the stable. Mrs. Farrell, short and stocky, was housekeeper and in charge of the staff. They were both in their forties, and had been employed by the Catons for six months with trumped up references.

The house was completely empty except for themselves. The Caton family was on their way to a farewell gathering at one of the neighbors, two miles away. The three daughters and the Baron left in one carriage and the parents in another. The personal servants of the nobility were housed in a nearby inn, and the servants of the house, under Mrs. Farrell, were off for the evening, but would return before dark.

Mr. and Mrs. Farrell looked at each other and smiled. There were three hours of daylight left, and they must be far away before nightfall. The couple had followed the Barnum's Hotel murder case in the newspapers and laughed together at the ineptness of the perpetrators, both now dead. The Farrells knew, to succeed, it had to be an inside job. Their past had been riddled with small time thievery wherever they had held a position. With the arrival of the three "American Graces," they had hit the jackpot.

Mr. Farrell also had his own safecracking tools, and diligently scrutinized Mr. Caton's safe whenever he had the opportunity. Tonight he was ready. All their belongings were packed and ready in their room. He had the small carriage and a pair of horses ready in the stable. All that was left to do was to open and empty the safe and hurriedly pack the jewelry in boxes. The goal was to get as far north to Delaware as possible before dark. He even had a coaching house in mind for the night.

None of the family would return before eleven. Darkness would delay any hue and cry before morning, and then it would take time for the police to mount a search. At dawn, with a change of horses, they would be gone from the coaching inn. Once into Delaware, the chase would become more difficult.

As her husband started on the safe, Mrs. Farrell brought the boxes, layered with towels, to the library near the safe. Then she returned upstairs and brought down their baggage. In twenty minutes the safe was opened, and he began handing the pouches and cases to his wife. Mrs. Farrell had been very observant of the jewelry on the women as they came down the stairs, and she silently cursed them because they had all decided to adorn themselves with some of their lesser diamonds, thus reducing the value of the loot.

She packed the boxes quickly and within an hour, the baggage and boxes were arranged in the carriage. As she left the house, she couldn't resist stuffing into her jacket pockets two elaborate sterling silver candle snuffers that she had taken a fancy to from the parlor and dining rooms.

The journey north went well for an hour until a sudden lurch sent Mr. Farrell almost over the edge of his seat while driving the carriage. Mrs. Farrell was thrust sharply against the inside of the door. Fortunately the carriage stayed upright. Mr. Farrell jumped from the driver's seat and opened the door for his angry wife. He suspected what had happened. The axle on one wheel had given way. What to do? This part of the road was in a more forested area. There were scattered horse farms, few houses and not an inn in sight.

"What are we going to do?" screamed his wife. "Can you fix it?"

"No, we have to abandon the carriage. I'll unharness the horses." He was trying to remain calm, not give in to panic. "We will have to walk until it is too dark or until we find an inn."

"Walk? Are you crazy? We can't carry everything!"

"I can lead the horses and carry one piece of baggage. You must carry the other bag."

"We can't leave the boxes here!" Her heart was thumping so hard, she thought she would collapse.

"Take out most of the clothes from the baggage and put the jewelry there instead. We will have to manage."

They pulled the baggage and boxes from the carriage and she did what he told her, cursing everything in sight, including her husband. They continued the journey on foot along the lonely road. They trudged on for almost an hour, the shadows lengthening, until they finally saw an inn in the distance.

"Keep yourself under control. Let me do the talking," said Mr. Farrell.

His wife went inside and he left the baggage with her, then led the horses to the stable, and saw them settled for the night. When he returned inside the inn, he explained the breakdown to the innkeeper, secured a room for the night, and booked an early morning stagecoach north. For what Mr. Farrell thought was a large fee, the innkeeper and his sons would get the carriage to the stable in the morning and repair it. Mr. Farrell told him it was crucial that they move on in the morning because they had a funeral to attend in Delaware. So far, so good.

After taking the baggage to their room, and freshening up, the Farrells returned to the dining room of the inn and ordered some late supper. They had registered under the name of Kelly. Each of them ordered a large gin from the bar and drank it quickly.

As they had passed through the dining room to their table, they had noticed a lone man sitting at a table. He noticed them also and wondered what the women had in each of her jacket pockets. Ornate silver handles gleamed in the firelight and they almost looked like small pistols. The man finished his meal and decided to wait in the lobby until they emerged from the dining room.

He opened a newspaper and waited. The innkeeper came over to him and asked if he intended to leave in the morning, and whether his search for the missing racehorse was getting anywhere.

"I covered the whole area today on horseback," the policeman, whose name was Officer Randall, replied in a low voice. "I believe the thief has moved on with the animal. Please keep it quiet. I had to ask you and your family questions, but your guests do not need to know who I am or why I am here. I will be leaving in the morning."

"Yes, sir. Seems a shame, a valuable horse like that. Who knows what kind of care it's getting."

"By the way," the policeman continued, "who are the latecomers in the dining room?"

"The Kellys? Their carriage broke down a way back on the road. We have to haul it in while they go to a funeral in Delaware tomorrow on the stagecoach."

"They seemed a bit unsettled." He didn't want to alarm the innkeeper by mentioning that the woman might be carrying a pair of pistols. The innkeeper returned to his duties and the policeman continued to wait.

At last the Farrells came through the lobby, and as they passed him in the chair, the policeman made a pretense of dropping the paper, and bending over and bumping against Mrs. Farrell to pick it up. He bumped her hard enough near her pocket that the candle snuffer fell out on the floor.

"What are you doing?" she shouted, her nerves on edge. "Give that to me!"

"Beg pardon, ma'am. Please forgive my carelessness." He reached down and picking up the silver piece, handed it to the irate woman.

Her husband looked at it in surprise, also wondering why it was in her pocket.

As they proceeded up the stairs, whispering, the policeman was very curious as to why she was carrying a pair of costly candle snuffers in her pockets.

At Brooklandwood, the servants returned about eight and found the Farrells gone with all their belongings. One of the men, Francis O'Brien, went out to the stable and saw that the small carriage and two horses were missing. Inside the house, the servants saw that everything looked normal throughout the rooms. O'Brien mounted a horse and rode to the nearby inn where the personal servants were staying. No one had seen the Farrells. He spoke with the innkeeper and asked him to send word to the police in the area by the early morning stagecoach, or someone on horseback. Mr. Caton of Brooklandwood was missing two servants, a husband and wife, who were suspected of stealing two horses and a carriage, and possibly other objects. Next he rode to the house where the farewell party was being held. O'Brien breathlessly asked for Mr. Caton to come to the door where he informed him of the situation.

"You did the right thing, O'Brien," Mr. Caton said, sadly shaking his head. "The police will come as soon as they can. I don't know what more we can do tonight." He glanced back to the rooms where the music and laughter floated into the hallway. "I don't want to spoil the party. We will be home soon."

Early in the morning, the Catons knew the full extent of the robbery, and waited impatiently for the police. Everyone in the house was shocked by the theft and behavior of the Farrells. Mr. Caton thought the safe had remained untouched; it was closed so carefully, but he was mistaken when the women wanted to return their diamonds.

At the inn, the Farrells were coming down the stairs with their baggage. Officer Randall was waiting for them. No longer did the woman carry candle snuffers in her pockets. She glared at the policeman as all three entered the dining room for breakfast. The northbound stagecoach would be leaving at nine.

Throughout breakfast, Office Randall wondered what was in the baggage along with presumably the candle snuffers. He followed the Farrells, or Kellys as he knew them, as they left the dining room and went into the lobby. There he heard a familiar voice talking to the innkeeper. It was a fellow policeman from the area named Benson. The two policemen conferred for a few moments. Officer Benson was heading to Brooklandwood, the Caton estate that was several miles away, because of the theft of two horses and a carriage, and possibly other objects by a couple who were employed at the house. He was checking the inns along the way for a suspicious couple, and had just been informed by the innkeeper that the carriage and horses were here in the stable. Officer Randall told Benson about the incident with the woman and the candle snuffers. They both decided to check the baggage of the Kellys.

When the policemen approached the Kellys, who were hovering around their baggage, the couple began to panic. The policemen identified themselves and asked the Kellys to open their baggage. Mr. Farrell stood motionless like he was in a state of shock, but Mrs. Farrell flew at the policemen, beating at them with her large, heavy purse. Her cursing rang through the lobby. Officer Benson held her down as a crowd gathered. Officer Randall opened both bags, and the Farrells were undone.

The next day, order and personal property having been restored, and the Farrells in custody, Becky Cunningham left early by stagecoach for Catonsville, and the MacTavish family. She was sorry to be saying goodbye to the Baron and Baroness, but on Sunday she would be seeing Joshua again at his home. An exchange had been arranged so that one of Emily's housemaids would accompany the Staffords to England. The girl was twenty and an orphan. Her name was Cynthia Myers. She was lovely, and wished to please her new mistress. She eagerly looked forward to the ocean voyage.

As Becky rode the southbound stagecoach to arrive at her destination, Cynthia passed her en route to Greenspring Valley in the northbound stagecoach.

The three noble sisters, Mary Ann, Louisa, Elizabeth, and the Baron, left with their personal servants for Baltimore and another night at Barnum's Hotel. In the morning they would sail for England. All wished for an uneventful and restful voyage.

The End

REFERENCES

Isaac M. Fein, *The Making of An American Jewish Community, The History of Baltimore Jewry From 1773 to 1920*, Jewish Historical Society of Maryland, Inc., 1985

Karen Falk and Avi Y. Decter, Editors, *We Call This Place Home, Jewish Life in Maryland's Small Towns*, The Jewish Museum of Maryland, 2002

George C. Keidel PhD, Ed H. Parkison, Editor, *Colonial History of Catonsville*, American Bicentennial Committee of Catonsville, Catonsville, Maryland, 1976

H. Ralph Heidelbach, *Village of Catonsville*, Historical Background, 1987

Caroline Young and Colin King, *Railways and Trains*, Usborne Publishing Ltd., London, England, 1991

Henry K. Sharp, *The Patapsco River Valley, Cradle of the Industrial Revolution in Maryland*, Maryland Historical Society, 2001

Margie H. Luckett, Editor and Publisher, *Maryland Women*, Baltimore, Maryland, King Brothers Inc. Press, 1937

Baltimore City Directory, 1835

History of the Baltimore Police Department 1797-1997, Turner Publishing Co., 1997

Mary Ellen Hayward and Charles Belfoure, *The Baltimore Rowhouse,* Princeton Architectural Press, 1999